'Why is it that e̶ succumb to the ̶a̶t̶t̶r̶a̶c̶t̶i̶o̶n̶ ̶be-tween us you act as if you ̶h̶a̶v̶e escaped a fate worse than death when the moment is inter-rupted?' Nina cried.

'You underestimate my feelings,' Rob said with a chill in his voice to match her own. 'I don't feel as if I've escaped an unpleasant fate at all. It's more like having had to pass by the entrance to heaven.'

'Then why…?'

'You know why. I've already told you.'

'The trouble with you, Rob,' she flared, 'is that you're too blinkered to see what's staring you in the face. You're letting the past threaten the future!'

Abigail Gordon is fascinated by words, and what better way to use them than in the crafting of romance between the sexes? A state of the heart that has affected almost everyone at some time in their lives. Twice widowed, she now lives alone in a Cheshire village. Her two eldest sons have between them presented her with three delightful grandchildren, and her youngest son lives nearby.

Recent titles by the same author:

FINGER ON THE PULSE
SAVING FACES
DR BRIGHT'S EXPECTATIONS

THE ELUSIVE DOCTOR

BY
ABIGAIL GORDON

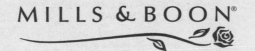

All the characters in this book have no existence outside the imagination of the author, and have no relation whatsoever to anyone bearing the same name or names. They are not even distantly inspired by any individual known or unknown to the author, and all the incidents are pure invention.

First published in Great Britain 2001
Harlequin Mills & Boon Limited,
Eton House, 18-24 Paradise Road, Richmond, Surrey TW9 1SR

© Abigail Gordon 2001

ISBN 0 263 82290 7

Set in Times Roman 10½ on 12 pt.
03-0201-48720

Printed and bound in Spain
by Litografía Rosés, S.A., Barcelona

CHAPTER ONE

AT MID-MORNING the main street of the village was busy. A smattering of those who lived in Stepping Dearsley were moving purposefully in and out of its few shops and the rest, who had come by car, bus and train, to spend a summer's day in one of Cheshire's prettiest villages, were engaged in a variety of pursuits. Morning coffee being one of them.

Those who thought themselves up-market were gravitating towards the lounge of the Royal Venison Hotel where peacocks strutted on smooth green lawns. Or to the quaint café next to the butcher's for those who either couldn't afford the hotel's prices or preferred a more chintzy atmosphere.

In a small courtyard close to the hotel a group of ramblers were eyeing the paintings in Sara Forrester's small art gallery, and when they moved away, with the studs of their walking boots clinking on cobbles which had been there longer than anyone could remember, a teacher and a party of schoolchildren out for the day took their place.

Across the way, the stone building which had once been a small church was taking in and spilling out those who had cause to seek the help and advice of their GP. And as Nina surveyed it from the opposite pavement her expression was no more cheerful than it had been since she'd arrived at the house that she could see gleaming whitely through the trees at the other end of the village.

This sunny backwater wasn't Kosovo, Bosnia or the

Sudan, she thought gloomily as a young mother, clutching a prescription with one hand and a whimpering toddler with the other, came out of the building that she herself would shortly be entering.

She'd had such plans, such idealistic ideas of what she'd been going to do when she'd qualified, and they'd all been centred around setting the world to rights.

And instead...what had happened? A letter in the post from her father to say that she'd been needed at home. The old tartar hadn't even said 'please', and if it had been anyone else but Eloise who'd been the cause of the abrupt summons to present herself in this place, miles from anywhere, she would have refused.

But if her dad was a pain, Eloise was her dearest friend, as well as her stepmother. The news that she'd been diagnosed as suffering from breast cancer had thrown Peter Lombard into a state of uncharacteristic panic, and in his usual autocratic way he'd ordered Nina to return to the fold.

He hadn't considered that she might have had other plans and, when Eloise had protested that she was all right and could cope with whatever the future held, he'd still been adamant that his daughter must be with them at such a time.

'There's a vacancy for a trainee GP here in the village,' he'd said when Nina had phoned in answer to his letter. 'So if they'll take you on, you won't stagnate.'

Stagnate? she'd wanted to cry. I'll suffocate in that place!

The thought of being cooped up in the country hideaway to which he and Eloise had moved only twelve months before gave her claustrophobia. She was a city girl. Nightclubs, discos, shopping malls—those were her scene.

She'd been the life and soul of the party amongst the medical students at the London university where she'd studied for her degree, and once she'd got it she'd been ready for off, only to be brought to heel by her father's summons.

Obviously she hadn't been going to refuse. Knowing her father, he would be worse than useless if things got really bad for Eloise, and his gentle wife, whose loving kindness had won the heart of a grieving eleven-year-old many years ago, would need her support.

Nina had arrived home the previous day and had known that her dad, in spite of his high-handed ways, on this occasion had been right. She and Eloise had clung to each other, and the young medical graduate had realised that their roles had been reversed. The mantle of the protector was now upon her shoulders.

Peter Lombard's suggestion that she find herself employment locally had been digested and reluctantly acted upon. Hence the fact that she was standing, glum-faced, outside this quaint stone edifice which was the centre of health care in Stepping Dearsley.

Bracing herself, Nina crossed over the street, and as she hesitated outside the surgery she groaned at the thought of what lay ahead.

An elderly woman passing by eyed her curiously. 'You all right, my dear?' she asked. 'I haven't seen you around here before. But, then, we get a lot of strangers in the place. We village folk sometimes feel that there's no room for us.'

'I'm Peter Lombard's daughter,' she told her, wondering why she had to identify herself to this old dear. 'He lives in the white house at the far end of the village.'

Bright old eyes twinkled up at her. 'Ah, so you belong

to one of the newcomers. You're family to that nice
Missus Lombard, then?'

Nina nodded. She saw no point in telling this old chat-
terbox that her mother had died when she was eleven
and that shortly afterwards her father had presented her
with a lovely stepmother.

What Eloise had ever seen in her father she didn't
know. He was ex-army and never forgot it. Not an easy
man to live with. But she supposed he was handsome in
his own way. Tall, supple still, hair of dark russet that
was now turning to silver and green eyes that didn't miss
a thing.

She had inherited his striking good looks and could
sometimes be just as strong-willed, but the basis of
Nina's character had come from her mother, and sometimes when she saw her father at his most awkward she
sent up a prayer of thanks for the breezy yet generous
confidence which had been her legacy from the woman
who'd been taken from them.

It wasn't in evidence today, though, far from it. She
was out on a limb in this place, like a wary creature out
of its habitat, and there wasn't a lot she could do about
it.

'I'm Kitty Kelsall,' the old lady was saying. 'Mine's
the end cottage there. I do a bit of cleaning at the surgery
but I've finished for today. They've got the decorators
in and there isn't much I can do until they've finished.'

'Oh, I see,' Nina commented absently. So she was
going to be interviewed by the members of the practice
surrounded by paint pots. Would they be chewing on
straws, she wondered...and dressed in smocks?

In whatever way the panel of GPs who were to interview her might be attired, at least *she* was looking her
best, Nina thought as she pushed open double glass

doors and slowly made her way into the Stepping Dearsley Group Practice.

In a smart suit of fine black wool, relieved with a white silk blouse, and her shining russet crop styled in a short cut which brought into focus her fine-boned face with its tilting mouth and challenging green eyes, she was feeling happy about her appearance, if nothing else.

She'd been right about one thing, she decided as she looked around her. The decor was certainly of a hay-stacks and buttercups type. Wooden settles were there for the waiting patients to sit on, rather than neat wooden chairs, and the wallpaper had a definite dated look about it.

But that atmosphere didn't follow through to the room from which a group of receptionists were eyeing her with smiling curiosity, and she thought that whatever the place lacked in glamour it made up for in numbers of staff. How many folk were there living in the village, for goodness' sake?

'I have an appointment with the partners,' she said coolly as one of the receptionists asked in what way she could help.

'Ah, I see,' the woman said. 'Two of them are on their rounds,' she explained, 'and the others are down-stairs.'

She pointed to a door next to where Nina was stand-ing. 'It's through there, Dr...er, Lombard, isn't it?'

'Yes, that's correct.'

'The focal point of the practice is downstairs,' the receptionist said, still bent on putting the interviewee in the picture. 'We have a large area below street level and all the computers are there, along with our admin staff.'

Nina found herself gaping slightly. The place looked like the old curiosity shop decor-wise, but it appeared to have a glut of receptionists and a computer terminal below stairs. Maybe it wasn't going to be as big a bore as she'd thought.

'Shall I show you the way?' the woman was asking.

Nina shook her head. 'No. I'll find my own way, thanks just the same. If I get lost I'll come back.'

If the upper floor of Stepping Dearsley Group Practice was not modern, the same couldn't be said of what lay beneath, Nina decided as she made her way along a recently decorated passage which led into a large chamber that looked more like the headquarters of a space launch than a doctor's surgery.

As she made her entrance one of the painters was putting the finishing touches to the paintwork of a cornice that ran the length of the room, but there was no one else in sight.

He hadn't seen her and when she said, 'Excuse me,' he whirled round on the scaffolding that was supporting him and caught the paint pot beside him.

It didn't hit her but it splashed as it fell, and as Nina gasped in dismay she thought that it would have to be white...and she would have to be wearing a black suit!

The man was looking down on her in stunned disbelief, and as she glared up at him she said the first thing that came into her head.

'And so what are you going to do about this?' she hissed, pointing to the splashes on her skirt. 'You're wearing white overalls. The paint wouldn't have shown on you. But, no, you have to go and spill it all over me! I've got an interview any moment in this rural backwater and what am I going to look like?'

'Pretty good, as far as I'm concerned,' he said slowly, as if he was finding his voice with difficulty. 'I really am sorry, but I'd no idea there was anyone around, and when you spoke it startled me.' Still standing on the plank, he pointed to a bottle on the floor beside her. 'We could try turps on it.'

'Would *you* like to attend an interview smelling to high heaven of white spirit?' she snapped. 'And, for goodness' sake, will you come down off there? My neck's beginning to ache with looking up.'

As he obeyed the request and jumped down off the scaffolding, Nina thought that he wasn't exactly prostrate with contrition. There was laughter in the brown eyes observing her from beneath the white cloth cap that went with the overalls.

'You could turn the skirt back to front,' he suggested, 'and even if you didn't, I'm sure that the doctors won't hold it against you.'

'I should hope not!' Nina exclaimed. 'It isn't my fault that I'm in this mess. I don't know what firm you're working for, but I think that your employer should be made to reimburse me for a new skirt. And speaking of the doctors, where are they? The receptionist said that there were some of them down here.'

'Yes, there are,' he said, but before he could explain further there was the sound of feet on the stairs and he began to unbutton the overalls.

'Rob!' an amazed female voice cried before he could divest himself of them. 'What are you up to?' It belonged to a willowy brunette with curves in all the right places and a heavily made-up face.

The decorator laughed. 'I was just touching up the cornice where they'd missed a bit.'

She sighed. 'You're crazy. What do you think we're paying them for?' Light hazel eyes had swivelled to where Nina was standing, nonplussed and paint-spattered.

'And you are…?' she questioned.

'Nina Lombard,' she said stiffly. 'I'm here to be interviewed for the doctor's vacancy in the practice—and I don't usually present myself covered in paint on this sort of occasion.'

'That's my fault, Bettine,' the man called Rob said. 'I knocked a can of paint over and you can see what happened.' He turned to a fuming Nina. 'I suppose I should introduce myself, Dr Lombard. It isn't Michelangelo that you see before you…or a member of Jarvis and Pendelbury, the local decorating firm who are transforming our premises. Robert Carslake, senior partner of Stepping Dearsley group practice at your service.'

The cap was in his hand and the overalls halfway off, and as she took in the sight of broad shoulders, trim flanks, dark brown hair and eyes the colour of winter chestnuts Nina broke into breathless laughter. What a beginning to a career in rural health. That was, if she got the job.

She got it, but not as easily as she might have expected. For one thing, the joker of the paint pots was a different person when seated behind a big oak desk flanked by his colleagues.

He was pleasant and polite, but Nina saw immediately that he was nobody's fool and she wondered if he was the big brain behind the outfit or if they all had equal status, although that wasn't likely if he was senior partner.

The curvy brunette, who had a noticeably proprietorial attitude towards him, was introduced to her as Bettine Baker. A fair-haired man of a similar age to herself, sitting beside Dr Baker, was called Gavin Shawcross, and seated at the other side of Robert Carslake was Dr

Vikram Raju, a middle-aged man of Asian origin, who was watching her with friendly dark eyes.

At which university had she taken her degree? Robert Carslake wanted to know. Where had she done her in-hospital training? Had she any plans to specialise, either now or in the future?

How long would she be available to work in the practice if they took her on? Bettine Baker asked with a noticeable lack of enthusiasm.

When Nina replied that it would be for as long as she was needed at home, Robert Carslake said with a smile that was somewhat tight around the edges, 'So you're prepared to work in this "rural backwater", as you described it, for as long as it suits you, but not necessarily to the advantage of ourselves?'

With the feeling that she had well and truly started off on the wrong foot, Nina flashed him a tentative smile of her own. 'I used that term in a moment of irritation.' Glancing down at the paint splashes on her skirt, she went on, 'You may recall that I'd just come into contact with a can of white paint.'

There was a sinking feeling in the pit of her stomach. Were she to confess that her angry description of Stepping Dearsley was indeed how she saw the place, her job prospects could fly out of the window and she couldn't afford that to happen.

The last thing she wanted was for her father to have to support her, or to have to seek employment other than in the health service. But these people, the doctors of the village's group practice, weren't to know that all her plans and hopes had been knocked sideways for the love of a sick woman…and at the command of a man who always expected to be obeyed.

Nina swallowed hard. 'I'm sorry if I've given you that

impression. If you offer me the chance to work in the practice I would hope to be a useful and dedicated member of your team. It would be my first position since graduating and obviously a great challenge. When I said that my home circumstances might dictate how long I was available I was thinking of my stepmother's illness, of which you are no doubt aware.'

'We know that you're Peter Lombard's daughter and that his wife has a health problem,' Robert Carslake conceded, 'but I'm sure you realise that our decision will be based on what is best for the practice.'

'Yes, of course,' she murmured meekly.

'And that we shall want to discuss the matter between ourselves before making a commitment.'

'Yes.'

He got to his feet and the atmosphere lightened. 'We'll be in touch in a couple of days, Dr Lombard. We can reach you at your parents' home, I presume?'

She would have liked to have said, yes, if she hadn't died from excitement first, but that would have gone down no better than her previous comment about the village. She was a city creature. These country dwellers weren't going to understand her frustrations.

Instead, she nodded with continuing meekness, and as they shook hands in farewell Nina knew that, last outpost of civilisation or not, she wanted the job.

As she climbed the stairs that would take her back to ground floor level and the consulting area of the practice, Robert Carslake caught up with her.

'I'll pay for dry-cleaning, or a new suit if necessary,' he offered in a low voice as she turned to face him, and added, with a smile that had more warmth in it than those he'd been displaying downstairs, 'I never can resist slapping a bit of paint on when the opportunity presents itself. It has much less chance of backfiring on one than treating the sick.'

Still with her snappy answer-back technique on hold, Nina smiled back. 'Thank you for the offer, Dr Carslake.' And with a swish of paint-daubed skirt and her high heels clicking noisily on the stone path outside the practice, she made her departure.

'So how did it go?' her father wanted to know the minute she stepped over the threshold, 'and whatever possessed you to go looking like that?'

His glance was on the white splashes and she sighed. 'In answer to your first question...not very well, I feel, and with regard to the second, I didn't go looking like this. The senior partner threw a can of paint over me.'

'Threw a can of paint over you!' he repeated, his jaw dropping. 'Good grief!'

'Well, maybe ''knocked'' would be a better description.'

'Don't tell me the fellow's doing his own decorating!' he growled. 'I'm aware that the place is being done up. Old Battersby, who ruled the roost before, has retired and Carslake's taken over as senior partner. There is a lot that needs doing, but decorating the place himself...!'

'He wasn't. Merely doing a bit of touching up.'

Peter Lombard frowned. 'I hope I understand that comment correctly.'

Nina laughed. It wasn't like her father to crack a joke, but if his expression was anything to go by he wasn't aware that he had.

'Where's Eloise?' she asked, bringing her mind to bear on what really mattered.

'Having a rest upstairs. She was feeling tired and nauseous.'

'Poor love. I'll go to her,' she said, and as he nodded in sombre agreement she went slowly upstairs.

Up to this point there had been no mention of a mastectomy for Eloise. The initial lump, having been found to be malignant, had been promptly removed and now she was enduring chemotherapy.

So far there were no signs that the cancer had spread but, on the dark side of it, both her mother and elder sister had died from the illness, which did make it more likely that her problems could be just beginning.

Of the three of them in the Lombard household the patient herself was the one least overwrought, and when Nina went into the sunlit bedroom where Eloise was resting the only emotions mirrored in her eyes were those of pleasure and affection.

'So tell me all about it,' she said as her stepdaughter perched on the edge of the bed.

'There isn't much to tell,' Nina confessed. 'Except that I said all the wrong things and got in the way of a would-be decorator.'

Eloise's pale face crumpled into laughter. 'I'm not sure whether I should pursue the matter on the strength of those admissions.'

'Tell me about Robert Carslake,' Nina said casually. 'Who is he? Where does he live, and so on?'

'He's thirty-five years old, recently promoted, senior partner of the village practice.'

'And?'

'At the moment he's living in a flat above the surgery. Regarding the ''and so on'' part of your question, I'm taking it that you want to know if he's spoken for?'

'Is he?'

''Fraid so,' Eloise said sympathetically. 'The man is engaged to one of the doctors in the practice.'

'And as they consist of a middle-aged man, a blonde stripling of the same sex and a sexy brunette with curves in all the right places, it isn't hard to guess which of them is wearing his ring,' Nina said ruefully. 'And as I'm not going to get the job…what does it matter?'

Eloise pushed a strand of gold hair, which was fast thinning, off her forehead, and patted her stepdaughter's hand gently. 'What will you do if you don't? You know that I don't want you to change all your plans because of me.'

'I know that,' Nina said softly, 'but charity begins at home, and even if my aspirations aren't in this place it's here that my heart is.'

A single tear rolled down her stepmother's hollow cheek. 'Bless you, darling Nina,' she said, and as the two women stayed silent, each with their own thoughts, the girl with the sad green eyes vowed that she would be prepared to wash dishes in the hotel kitchen if no other work were available, just as long as she could be with Eloise…and didn't have to be supported financially by her father.

'What have you done about the skirt?' a voice asked from behind Nina as she queued for stamps in the village post office the following morning.

When she swung round Robert Carslake was there. This time he was in the relaxed guise of the countryman, in a fine checked shirt, open at the neck to display a strong, tanned neck, corduroy trousers, sitting snugly on trim hips, and a pair of soft leather boots on his feet.

'You're not treating the sick…or decorating this morning, then?' she enquired innocently as their glances held for a moment.

'No. It's my day off,' he replied blandly. 'We're going into town to do some shopping.'

She sighed melodramatically. 'Lucky you. How I long for the carbon-monoxide fumes, the grind of the traffic, the summer sales... I could go on for ever!'

'Really?' he commented with raised eyebrows. 'So, as you were at pains to point out yesterday, you're not impressed with our beautiful village?'

'I can live with it...or in it, I should say,' she said hurriedly, wishing once again that she'd kept quiet. 'If you don't give me a job in the practice, I'll find something else to do. I saw in the parish magazine last night that they're advertising for a verger,' she added, her green eyes dancing.

He shuddered. 'Maybe we'd better give you a job, then. I'd hate church services to have to suffer because *we* weren't prepared to.'

'What—suffer?'

He was looking her over, his brown eyes taking in her tight black pants, the skimpy halter top covering high-thrusting breasts and the narrow waist that he could have almost spanned with his two hands.

The thought of having this pert young trainee as part of his team was crazy, and yet he was prepared to risk it. He wasn't going to ask his colleagues to change their minds about the decision they'd made after she'd left the previous day.

What mattered was how good a doctor she was. Her views on everyday matters didn't count. As long as she pulled her weight in the practice and knew what she was about, he would be satisfied.

As a graduate she would be answerable to one of them as her trainer and, though Gavin Shawcross had been champing at the bit to volunteer for the duty, for some reason he'd found himself informing them that he was going to take her under his wing.

Gavin had given in with reasonably good grace, Vikram had nodded his smiling agreement and Bettine's mouth had tightened angrily for some reason or other, but it had made no odds.

For good or bad, they were going to take Nina Lombard on, and maybe when she'd had a taste of village life she would stop beefing about this heavenly corner of the Cheshire countryside.

'So when will I know if I'm to be taken off the list of the nation's unemployed?' she was asking.

He could have told her there and then, but the crowded post office was hardly the place to discuss practice matters. So, keeping to the arrangement he'd intended, Rob Carslake said smoothly, 'I'll pop round this evening to give you our decision.'

It would do this extremely confident young madam no harm to stew for a few hours, he thought as he made his way to where a still displeased Bettine was waiting for him.

The trip into town hadn't been a success. For one thing, Bettine should have been on duty. But because it was his day off she'd insisted on coming with him, and although he'd finally given in to her wheedling he hadn't been happy to think that she was trying to pull rank because they were engaged.

And on the heels of that thought had come another. Why hadn't she wanted them to take on another doctor? They had seven thousand patients registered with them. Renowned for its excellence, the practice served other nearby villages and even borderline parts of the town.

That meant that the workload was heavy, the paperwork vast, hence the computer room downstairs. Unless they were making an error of judgement, Nina Lombard's addition to the team could only ease the burden.

The two previous times Rob had seen her she'd been wearing black, a colour greatly favoured by the young female of the species, he'd thought. Having expected a repetition, he was surprised to find her in a yellow sundress and strappy sandals to match when he called at the Lombard house early that evening.

As he pulled up on the drive Rob saw a flash of gold in the shrubbery and, knowing that he had business with both the women of the house, he went to find out which of them it was standing silently, gazing into space across the green meadows that encircled the village.

It only needed a glance to tell him that it was the younger of the Lombard women that he was approaching, and until a twig snapped beneath his feet, bringing her round to face him, he could have been forgiven for thinking her a statue.

So she was capable of stillness, he thought illogically. Nina Lombard wasn't always restless and questioning. Was her reverie one of boredom, or loneliness, or grief maybe? That emotion might be something that the future held for the autocratic ex-soldier and the confident young trainee he was shortly going to be working with.

Whatever she'd been ruminating on, it was the girl who'd dodged the paint can who was observing him now, and there was no mistaking the question in her eyes.

'The job is yours if you want it, Nina,' he said quietly. 'So what do you say?'

She smiled. 'I say, yes, please...er, Dr Carslake.'

'Good. That's settled, then. If you'd like to come in to see me tomorrow, we'll discuss salary and a starting date. And now I'd like to see your mother. It's not an official visit, but as I'm here already I'd like a quick chat, just to see how she's coping with the chemotherapy.'

'Yes, of course. And Eloise is my stepmother… although she's always been like a mother to me.'

He smiled and she thought crazily that he had a lovely mouth. At least it was when he wasn't putting her in her place, and she wondered how many times he was going to have to do that in the near future.

'So you're taking my daughter into the camp,' her father said with gruff gratification when they went into the house. 'You'll find she's a chip off the old block.'

'And what exactly does that mean, sir?' Robert Carslake enquired blandly with an amused glance at Nina's grim expression.

'Ready to take orders. Keeps her kit in good condition. Not frightened of a bit of footslog, and there's plenty of that to be had amongst these hills and dales.'

'Yes, I'm sure you're right,' the other man agreed in the same smooth tone, 'and we shall look forward to having her with us. Now maybe I could have a word with your wife. Is she around?'

'Of course she's around,' he barked. 'Where would you expect her to be with what she's got? Feels sick all the time and hasn't any energy.'

Robert Carslake watched Nina turn away. So that was the way of it. This lively young woman was here to support the sick—not just in her stepmother's illness but also as a buffer against this old martinet's insensitivity.

He'd probably never had a day's illness in his life and didn't know how to cope with someone who had.

When Nina saw him to the door he paused on the point of leaving. Anxious to take away the mortification showing so clearly in the beautiful green eyes, Rob said jokingly, 'I'll believe it when I see you taking orders, and as for your kit, it's not everyone who walks about covered in paint, but the best bit was the footslog. I thought you townies just jumped out of one taxi into another. Or do you have a car?'

'Yes, I have a car,' she replied. 'A red Mini.'

'So with a bit of luck we won't lose you when we send you out into the backwoods?'

'Don't bank on it,' she said flatly, her father's humiliating commendation still rankling.

CHAPTER TWO

WHEN her father called upstairs at half past eight the next morning Nina buried her head in the pillow. She'd been up most of the night with Eloise. It had only been when the older woman's discomfort had at last lessened, and she'd drifted off to sleep on the sofa in the lounge, that Nina had crept upstairs as the summer dawn had been breaking.

'Come along, lazybones,' he was calling. 'Dr Carslake is on the phone for you.'

'All right! All right!' she grumbled as she picked up the bedside phone.

'Robert Carslake here, Nina,' his voice said in her ear. 'Can you come in to see me about twelvish? That's the best time for me, between the end of surgery and starting my rounds.'

'Yes,' she mumbled.

There was a moment's silence and then he asked, 'Have I got you out of bed?'

'No,' she informed him with drowsy honesty. 'I'm still in it.'

'I see. Well, that will soon be changing, I'm afraid.'

She stifled a yawn. 'Yes, I suppose so, but the reason for me still being half-asleep at this hour won't.'

'Eloise had a bad night?'

'Mmm. I'm afraid we were burning the midnight oil just a bit.'

'And your father, too?'

'No, not Dad. If he'd had a broken night he might

23

have slept through reveille and that would never have done.'

She had a feeling that he was smiling at the other end of the phone and, instead of feeling gratified, she felt guilty. Her father couldn't help the way he was.

'So I'll see you, then,' Robert Carslake said in a voice that showed that he was well and truly awake.

'Yes, sir!' she said, and sank back against the pillows.

Nina's second visit to the surgery was by no means as depressing as the first. This time a different receptionist showed her to a consulting room on the ground floor, and when she knocked on the door and ushered Nina inside Robert Carslake was sitting behind the desk. Today he was dressed in a smart grey suit and looking just as easy on the eye.

If he thought the same about her he gave no sign, merely enquiring if she was now fully awake.

'Yes, I am,' she told him briskly, 'and raring to go.'

Where to she wasn't quite sure, but if it boosted his confidence in her the comment would have been worth it.

When they'd finished discussing the details of her employment Robert Carslake said, 'You met my partners yesterday, and I'm sure that you'll get along with all three. Dr Raju is a very pleasant man and will be only too pleased to help should you experience difficulties of any kind. So also will Gavin Shawcross. Bettine Baker is also a very competent doctor.'

'Yes, I'm sure she is,' Nina murmured, noting that he hadn't included his fiancée amongst those who would be happy to assist her. Neither had he explained their relationship. But why should he? The man's private life was his own affair, she supposed.

'And as for myself,' he went on calmly, 'you might feel that you have me at your elbow more than you would like as I'll be in charge of your training here.

'Whenever we employ someone like you, which we frequently do, it's an extra role that I take on. I'm perfectly qualified to do so.' He was smiling and she thought again what an attractive mouth he had. 'And I hope that you'll find your time here interesting and profitable.' The smile was widening. 'In spite of your aversion to the countryside.'

'I'd like to start as soon as possible,' she said, not rising to the bait. 'Dad is there for Eloise during the day so it will pose no problem. It's during the night that she needs me the most.'

'There could be others who'll need you during those hours also,' he reminded her.

'Yes, I do know that, and I can manage without sleep. You just caught me at a drowsy moment this morning. Probably the change of air or sleeping in a strange bed.'

'Maybe,' he said, absently drumming his fingers on the desktop. 'But in any case, in the beginning I'll accompany you on any night calls that the emergency help line has to pass on to us.

'So, would you like to start tomorrow? As far as the practice is concerned, there's no reason why not, if you're as keen to get settled in as you say.'

It wasn't that she was keen, Nina thought. It was more a situation of having to swallow a pill and knowing that delaying the moment would solve nothing.

The fact that this particular pill was offering a very pleasant coating in the form of the man who was going to be her trainer had to be an unexpected bonus.

'Had you visualised starting your work as a doctor in a rural practice?' he asked curiously when they'd confirmed that she would report for duty at eight o'clock the following morning.

'Not exactly,' she said evasively.

If he were to discover just how much she'd wanted to go overseas he might feel that he ought to look elsewhere for someone more enthusiastically inclined towards working in Stepping Dearsley's group practice, and if he did that what would she do?

Whether she liked it or not, here she was to stay—at least for the time being. Maybe one day, if and when Eloise had fought off the silent killer, she would realise her dream.

A knock on the door broke into the moment, and the willowy Dr Baker came in. She gave Nina a vague sort of smile and then, as if that had dealt with her presence, said, 'Are we lunching together, Rob?'

He frowned. 'I doubt it. I've got a lot of calls on my list.'

She tapped her foot irritably. 'What about Gavin and Vikram? Can't they take some of them?'

No mention of easing the burden herself, Nina noted.

He shook his head. ''Fraid not. They've enough on their hands as it is. It's this summer flu bug that's going around.'

'Yes, I do know that there's yet another virus keeping us busy,' she said snappily. 'I suppose I could take some of your calls if it means we can snatch a few moments together.'

Nina eyed her in surprise. So much for making snap judgements.

'Whatever,' he conceded easily. 'I'll meet you in the Royal Venison for a quick snack about twoish.' With hia voice tightening somewhat, he added, 'Does that suit you?'

'Yes, darling,' she cooed.

Nina was beginning to feel decidedly surplus to requirements, and Robert Carslake switched his attention back to her. 'So we'll see you tomorrow then, Nina.'

'So soon?' Bettine exclaimed. 'You must be keen!'

'Perhaps you've forgotten just how hard-up medical students can be, Dr Baker,' Nina said levelly. 'Or maybe there were more generous grants in your day.'

And if that isn't going to make me an enemy before I've even started, I don't know what will, she thought defiantly. What was wrong with the woman, for goodness' sake? Surely she wasn't displeased because they'd taken a woman younger than herself into the practice.

The sophisticated Dr Baker would have no competition coming from her direction—a wet-behind-the-ears trainee who was going to need all the help she could get, both in the practice and outside it.

There were just two receptionists on duty when Nina presented herself the next morning. It seemed that the others were either on holiday or it was their day off.

'There are five of us altogether,' a friendly, middle-aged blonde said when the young doctor hesitated in front of a counter that had a backdrop of countless shelves filled with patient records.

She held out a ringless hand. 'I'm Barbara Walker—and you're the new doctor, aren't you? I saw you yesterday when you came to see Dr Carslake.'

Nina smiled and hoped that it came over as a confident beam because she was feeling anything but relaxed. Right up to the moment she'd parked her Mini at the back of the practice she'd had no qualms about the day ahead, but the moment she'd stepped inside panic had set in.

Suppose she did something stupid. Made herself look a complete fool in front of a patient or, worse still, in the presence of Robert Carslake... Or, even more dreadful than that, when the unfriendly Bettine was around.

'The other doctors haven't arrived yet,' Barbara was saying. 'Shall we go into the kitchen for a coffee? Kitty, the cleaner, always brews up for us before we start.'

'Yes, please,' Nina told her. 'I'd love a coffee.'

She'd eaten the porridge her father made for breakfast all the year round and had drunk a cup of strong black tea. 'Get it down you, girl,' he'd ordered. 'It might be the only rations you'll get all day.' But she preferred to start off with a coffee and hoped that she might feel more sprightly after the caffeine intake.

The elderly woman that she'd chatted with on the day of her interview eyed Nina in surprise when she followed the receptionist into the kitchen.

'Well, I never!' she exclaimed. 'So you're the new doctor! There was me thinking you were just visiting your folks.'

If Nina had wanted to explain that had indeed had been the case, she didn't get the chance. The door had just opened to admit Robert Carslake and the woman he was engaged to.

When he saw her leaning against one of the kitchen units with a cup of the steaming brew in her hand, he said easily, 'Hi, there. I see that you're being looked after.'

'Yes, thanks,' she replied in a tone that was polite but not servile.

The woman at his side said nothing. She didn't need to. Her expression said it all—that this young trainee needed taking down a peg or two, that the girl was too confident for her own good.

But Nina thought, I'm not a girl. I'm twenty-seven years old, and just because Bettine Baker is about ten years ahead of me it doesn't mean that I'm still in ankle socks. Maybe she isn't so sure of brown-eyed Rob, and wants to keep him all to herself. Well, she was welcome. He might be a very presentable member of the opposite sex, but a country GP wasn't what she, Nina Lombard, was looking for.

The moment her first patient walked into the small room that Rob had given her adjoining his, Nina's natural resilience asserted itself.

She'd done six-month stints on hospital wards during her training, dealing with the public all the time. This wasn't a great deal different, except for the surroundings and the fact that she was on her own, facing the patient in a one-to-one situation.

If she got stuck, the charismatic Rob was at the other side of the communicating door, ready to listen and advise, while one of the practice nurses, Judith Clark, a thirty-year-old divorcee, was in the room at the other side in case any of Nina's patients needed her services.

'I've been having tests done for a bladder problem,' the sixty-year-old woman who'd settled herself in the chair opposite was saying dourly. 'Have you got experience of that sort of thing?'

'Yes. I think I can say that.'

'You think!'

'I have,' Nina told her with a reassuring smile as she rephrased her answer. 'I've worked in the urology department at an infirmary during my training, and if by any chance you ask me something I don't know the answer to, Dr Carslake will come and sit in with me.'

The woman bridled at the suggestion. 'I'm not discussing my waterworks with a man. It was either you or Dr Baker, and she wasn't free.'

I'll bet she wasn't, Nina thought grimly. This was her first patient and she'd been hand-picked.

'Fine,' she said calmly. 'If you don't want Dr Carslake to see you, he won't. So, are you going to tell me what the problem is?'

'Huh!' the woman snorted. 'It's supposed to be the other way about. You're here to tell me what's wrong.'

'You misunderstand me,' Nina explained patiently. 'I'm asking you why you're here. You say that you've been having tests, but there's no paperwork amongst your records other than a copy of Dr Baker's letter asking for an appointment with a urologist.'

'And who's to blame for that, then?' the patient snapped.

'What sort of tests have you had?' Nina asked.

'Cystoscopy, kidney X-ray and an ultrasound.'

'When?'

'First you should be asking me why.'

'I don't need to ask you why,' she told her with continuing patience. 'It's here in the letter Dr Baker sent to the hospital. She found blood in your urine. So, tell me, when did you have the tests?'

'Last week. I've come for the results.'

'It can take up to two weeks for test results to come through,' Nina told her now that the reason for the woman's presence had been revealed, 'and once we receive them one of the doctors will ask to see you.'

She couldn't resist adding, 'Probably Dr Baker, as it was she who sent you for the tests in the first place.'

The ungracious one was getting to her feet. 'I might prefer to see you. Maybe you *do* know what you're talking about.'

When she'd gone Nina rolled her eyes heavenwards. What a start to her illustrious career at the Stepping Dearsley Group Practice. And what a dirty trick on Bettine Baker's part to pass that woman on to her.

The communicating door opened at that moment and Rob came in.

'I heard some of that,' he said apologetically. 'I don't know how you came to get Ethel Platt on your first day. She's head of our list of "handle with care" patients. But well done, anyway, Nina. Let's hope that the rest are easier to handle.'

They were. Mothers with grizzly teething babies, who seemed to have no gripe because they were being seen by the new doctor. A husky farm labourer who'd cut his hand quite badly on a machinery blade and made no demur when she had to send him further afield to the nearest casualty department. And an assortment of people who were sickening for the summer virus that was keeping the doctors busier than usual.

When the waiting room had been cleared Rob called her to one side. 'I'm taking you with me on my rounds,' he said. 'I don't want you to go on your own just yet. For one thing you need to know the area a bit better before you do that, and for another I want to see you in action on the home front.'

She pulled a wry face. 'Please, don't use army phraseology. My dad does it all the time.'

Rob laughed. 'The old guy still thinks he's in the barracks, does he? What was he? Sergeant?'

Nina threw up her hands in mock horror. 'Nothing so humble! He was a major in the Cheshires...and never lets us forget it.'

'Are you an only child?' he questioned.

'Yes. My mother died when I was eleven and shortly

afterwards Dad married Eloise. We lived in army quarters for a long while. I escaped by going to study medicine in London.'

'But have now been ordered back into service?'

'Is it that obvious?'

'Yes, I'm afraid so. Unlike the rest of us, you're not living in our beautiful village from choice. What were your original plans when you qualified and before your stepmother became ill?'

'Something more exciting than this, that's for sure.'

'Such as what?' he asked. 'Remember that excitement, fulfilment and a lot of other gratifying emotions often come from who one is with, rather than where one is.'

He picked up his bag with an abrupt movement. 'Come on, the day will be gone before we know it, and those who are suffering as they await us won't thank us for dawdling. You can tell me about your exciting plans another time.'

'So you're not lunching with Dr Baker today?' Nina asked mock-innocently, wanting to hit back for having her dreams dealt with so summarily.

Rob was still edgy. 'I won't even be having lunch, and neither will you, if we don't get a move on. We have to be back for afternoon surgery, you know.'

'I can't function without food,' she protested. 'I can cope with thirst, lack of sleep, but hunger...no!'

'You'll have to before you've done in this job, my girl. So be prepared.'

'Maybe I should start bringing iron rations.'

Rob threw back his head and laughed. 'Who's doing it now?'

'What?'

'Military jargon.'

Nina joined in the laughter. 'You see, it's catching.'

He had his hand on the doorhandle, waiting for her to precede him outside, and suddenly he was serious. 'Some things are, and once caught aren't so easily thrown off.'

His gaze was curiously intent and Nina felt her face start to burn. What did he mean? Was he referring to Bettine, who was waving to him from inside a low-slung Jaguar as she pulled away from the practice, *en route* to her share of the day's visits, or had it something to do with herself?

Tom Blackmore had advanced Parkinson's disease. It was at a stage that Nina had never before witnessed, and as she observed the old man's set expression and uncontrollable tremors it was hard to believe what Rob had told her about the patient before they'd gone into the remote farmhouse.

Tom had been one of the most successful farmers in the area, he'd said. A big, healthy man, who'd never known a day's sickness until he'd contracted the debilitating illness.

'Luckily, his sons have been there to see to the running of the farm,' he'd explained as they'd crossed the farmyard, 'and Mary, his wife, has nursed him with complete devotion, but now he's got to the stage where nothing seems to help—not the drugs he's on, or anything else. Levodopa was helpful for a long time but its benefits have ceased to exist as the illness has progressed.'

'There is some degree of dementia now, although he does have periods of lucidity, but his speech is affected and it's hard to understand what he's saying.'

'And how long do you think he's got?'

'Parkinson's is a slow killer,' he'd said in a low voice

as a plump, smiling woman in a floral apron had opened the door to them.

She'd been baking. There was a wire rack covered in hot scones in the middle of the kitchen table and Rob smiled as he saw Nina's eyes fasten on them.

He'd omitted to tell her earlier that Tom's wife always brewed up and offered a bite to go with it when they called, and, sure enough, after he'd introduced the new member of the practice Mary reached for a slab of farm butter and said, 'I'll be making you a bite to eat, Doctor, whilst you're examining my Tom.'

As they climbed the stairs he said softly, 'So you see, Dr Lombard, you don't have to endure hunger pains after all.'

The farmer eyed them questioningly when they entered the bedroom and Nina thought that here was a brain, functioning haphazardly, that was locked up in a suffering body.

She stood respectfully to one side as Rob examined him, noting the facial immobility and all the other distressing symptoms, and when they went back downstairs she wasn't surprised to hear him say to the farmer's wife, 'Would you like Tom to go away for a while to give you a rest, Mary? In a hospice maybe?'

The woman shook her head. 'No. I've managed this far, Doctor. I'm not going to leave him now.'

Rob nodded. 'Fair enough but, remember, you have only to give me a call if you change your mind.'

'I won't be doing that,' she said quietly as she put a plate of scones in front of them.

When they got outside Nina took a deep breath. It had been hot inside the farmhouse, and she guessed that it was for the sick man's sake as there would be little body heat coming from his trembling frame.

But she wasn't just drinking in the cool outside air for that reason. She'd joked with the man beside her about missing the carbon monoxide of the city, without admitting that here in the countryside the air was clear and sparkling, as were the waters of the small stream that was splashing past their feet.

'Watch it!' the man at her side warned with an amused smile as she breathed in yet again. 'Your lungs aren't used to being filled with pure air. You'll be confusing them.'

'Huh!' she mocked. 'It will take more than a few breaths of fresh air to convert me.' But as they got back into his car, which was a much less prestigious model than that of his fiancée, Nina felt a strange sense of completeness about the moment.

A week ago the man beside her had been merely a signature on a letter, asking her to attend an interview. She'd met him in person just three days ago and…what?

She was suddenly so aware of him she could hardly breathe. That was bad enough, but what was even worse was that he was engaged to be married and, tough townie though she might be, stealing other women's men was not on her agenda.

Rob had seen her expression and asked, 'What's wrong? First-day fatigue?'

'No, of course not,' she replied breezily. 'This is a refreshing change from working on the wards.'

'Really?' he remarked drily. 'You'll have to hope that it stays that way, then, although I wouldn't bank on it.'

Nina was scarcely listening. She didn't want to be making casual chit-chat. There was a desire in her to know all about him. Hadn't Eloise said he lived over the surgery? Why was that? she wondered. Maybe it was costing a lot to modernise the practice. Or perhaps he had a secret vice…drink or gambling.

He must be getting married some time in the future. Perhaps he and the unfriendly Bettine were saving up to buy a house and, from what she'd seen of his prospective bride, it wouldn't be a 'two up, two down'.

'I believe you live over the surgery?' she said casually. 'Doesn't it make you feel a bit too accessible, living on top of the job?'

He took his gaze off the road for a second and turned to face her. She saw mild surprise in his eyes. 'Yes, it does, but it has advantages, too. I don't have to travel to work for one thing, and for another it's economical.'

'Are you saving up to get married, then?' she probed.

'That and other things,' he said, and his tone told her that was the end of the discussion.

'Our next call is more central,' he said as they headed back for the village. 'Sara Forrester has asked me to call and see her. We have a problem with our local art dealer. She's agoraphobic and, even for a minor ailment, will ask for a visit rather than venture out.'

Remembering the small gallery beside the hotel, Nina asked curiously, 'If that's the case, how does she communicate with the artists?'

'They have to come to her. She doesn't go out looking for talent.'

'I wonder what's wrong with her today?' she wondered aloud, 'and what are we doing about the agoraphobia?'

'There isn't a lot we can do. The solution is in her own hands. It all started when she was mugged in the town one night, and since then Sara has been afraid to venture out.'

'Poor thing,' Nina said. 'She lives in this close-knit

community which, I imagine, is as safe as anywhere and then that happens.'

Rob smiled. 'We have our crimes here just as any-where else. They may be fewer in number because there are fewer of us to be robbed, but don't kid yourself that this is a crime-free place.'

The owner of the art gallery, an elderly woman with a nervous manner, hadn't called them out for a minor ailment. They found her lying on sweat-soaked sheets with a serious chest infection.

'You've got pneumonia, Sara,' Robert told her, 'and as there's no one to look after you I'm going to have you admitted to hospital.'

When the ambulance had been and gone with the sick woman inside it he said, 'It was a measure of how ill she was feeling that Sara didn't protest about being moved out of the house. Maybe after this enforced stay in the outside world her problem will be solved. In the meantime, this place will have to be closed until she's well again.'

By the time they'd finished the rest of the calls the afternoon was well upon them, and with the replenish-ment of her hunger seemingly in the distant past Nina was driven to mention food again.

He sighed. 'Is that all you think of? I'll drop you off at the café for a quick bite if you like before afternoon surgery.'

'Aren't you coming?'

Rob shook his head. 'No. I'll see you back at the practice. Vikram has a problem with one of his patients and I said we'd have a chat about it this afternoon.'

It was true. He had promised Dr Raju that he would help with the matter that was worrying him, but Rob

knew that wasn't the reason he'd opted out of eating
with Nina.

He'd had no qualms about introducing her into the
practice and now, before she'd even been employed
there a day, he was having second thoughts. Not about
her abilities. She'd got the hang of things pretty well so
far. It was the effect she was having on him that was
bothering him.

He was aware of every movement she made. The way
she moistened her lips with a small pink tongue before
she said something outrageous. The swaying of her hips
inside the straight black skirt as she walked. The swell
of her breasts inside her sweater. The candid green pools
of her eyes. He could go on for ever.

Was there a man in her life? he wondered. Some guy
who was as fond of city life as she was? Just as he
himself was engaged to a woman who loved the countryside as much as he did?

Hell! Surely that wasn't the only reason he'd let himself get entangled with Bettine. Of course it wasn't! She
was attractive, good at her job, fun to be with—some of
the time—but of late he'd had doubts as to whether he
wanted her to be the mother of his children—or to be
his wife for that matter. It was a measure of his unease
that he'd just thought of himself as entangled rather than
engaged.

One thing was for sure, he'd made a mistake nomi-
nating himself to train Nina Lombard. They would be
too much in each other's company, and although he
could very easily get to like that, he knew that Bettine
wouldn't.

But to alter the arrangements now would result in
questions being asked, and he didn't want that. It would

be better to leave things as they were…while keeping Dr Lombard in her place.

Eloise had cooked the evening meal. She was feeling less nauseous than on previous days and Nina's face lit up when she saw her dishing out the food.

The moment she heard her stepdaughter's light step on the kitchen floor tiles she swung round. 'How did it go?' she asked immediately.

Nina smiled. 'Fine. I started off with what must be the village's most crabby patient, but the rest of them were all right, and I've been doing the visits with ravishing Rob.'

Eloise laughed. 'Don't let your father hear you talking so flippantly about your superiors. He'll have you put in the glasshouse…and there's no telling what Dr Baker would do if she heard you.'

'Drag him off to the altar, maybe?'

'I don't know about that, but most of us in the village think that he's in no hurry to tie the knot.'

'How long have they been engaged?'

'Six months or so.'

Her father came stomping in at that moment, and now it was his turn to ask how her day had gone. Once she had answered a spate of questions that were fired at her like bullets, they sat down to eat.

When the meal was over and they'd cleared away, her father and Eloise went to sit in the garden, leaving Nina to prowl around the house like a caged animal.

It was at this time of day that she missed her town life. Tuning in to her restlessness Eloise suggested, 'Why not go to the pub for an hour?'

'The Royal Venison?'

She shook her head.

'No. Not the hotel. There's a small public house at the far end of the village. It's called the Gun and Target. That's where most of the lively ones congregate in the evenings.'

'You don't mind?' Nina asked, her glance taking in the sick woman's frailty.

'Of course not. I've got Peter here for company and I'll be going to bed shortly. The last thing I want is for you to feel that you have to be tied to the house.'

'Promise that you'll call me if you're not well in the night,' Nina said, hesitating in the doorway.

'I promise,' Eloise said, 'and now be off with you.'

CHAPTER THREE

NINA was surprised to see that the village was quite lively for a week night as she walked slowly along its main street.

There were cars on the forecourt of the hotel and through its long windows she could see people chatting in groups with drinks in their hands at what was obviously some sort of social gathering.

There were strollers along the riverside and a couple of young boys were riding up and down on the tarmac at the side of the surgery on what looked like new BMX bikes.

The floodlights of the art gallery, closed in the absence of its owner, were breaking up the gloom of the small square that stood in the shadow of the hotel, and as a hazy moon patrolled the sky in the summer dusk Stepping Dearsley didn't seem such a dull place after all.

When the Gun and Target came into sight there was so much activity going on around it that with a lifting of her spirits she thought it would put a bar in the city centre to shame.

Eloise had been right when she'd said that this was where the action was. Canned music blared into the night as an assortment of its patrons lounged outside at tables and chairs on a stone forecourt, and when she glanced through one of the mullioned windows it looked as if there wasn't a seat to be had.

She was turning away when her glance rested on what

was becoming a familiar profile. Rob Carslake was seated at a table in the corner with his fiancée, who was holding forth on some subject or other while he listened with only moderate interest.

So much for an evening in the pub, Nina decided glumly as she turned away. She'd spent the day with him. The last thing he would expect, or want, would be for her to be hovering out of working hours.

About to beat a speedy retreat, she found herself colliding with someone else who was checking up on just how full the place was. As his arm came out to steady her, she thought that it only needed the presence of Dr Raju, and the full contingent of the GPs from the Stepping Dearsley Practice would be there.

'Nina!' Gavin Shawcross said as he released her arm. 'You're not going already, are you?'

'Yes, I am. Actually, I've only just arrived, but the place is so crowded...and I've just spotted Robert Carslake and Bettine Baker inside.'

The fair-haired GP frowned. 'So?'

'So I think he'll have seen enough of me for one day.'

'That doesn't apply to me, though, does it? We've been introduced and that's about all.'

A table on the forecourt had just been vacated and, pointing to it, he said, 'Let me buy you a drink. It's time we got acquainted.'

She wanted to refuse. The magic of the summer night had gone the moment she'd seen the lovers, but what would she do if she did leave? Go back home to find her dad polishing his medals and Eloise in bed? Or sit out here on her own, not knowing a soul?

He was waiting for an answer and, seating herself, she

smiled up at him. 'Thanks. As you say, we need to get acquainted.'

'So how did your first day go?' he asked when he returned to the table with a bottle of wine and two glasses.

She laughed. 'That's what everyone wants to know. It went all right, thank you. It was interesting, challenging and...revealing.'

He noticed her hesitation and asked curiously, 'Revealing? In what way?'

'In all sorts of ways,' she said obliquely, having no intention of explaining that the life of a country doctor had proved more stimulating than she'd expected and that, far more important, so had the GP in whose company she'd been.

Rob came into view at that moment with Bettine beside him, her hand possessively on his arm, and Nina tensed. She was supposed to be avoiding him and yet where had she placed herself? In full view of anyone coming or going!

He saw them immediately and his face went blank, but he came over, with his companion reluctantly following.

'Hello, there. Relaxing after the day's toil, are we?' he said with cool pleasantness.

The question was addressed to them both but Nina sensed that it was aimed at her, and before Gavin Shawcross could get a word in she said airily, 'You've got it in one. I was thinking that we're only short of Dr Raju and we'd have the full monty.'

'So you knew that we were inside?' he questioned.

'Er...yes. I saw you through the window.'

'And doubtless realised that we wouldn't want to be disturbed,' the woman on his arm said sweetly.

'Yes, that's correct,' Nina agreed, 'and then I bumped into Gavin and here we are.'

'That being so, we'll leave you to get acquainted,' her trainer said with a stretched sort of smile. 'See you both in the morning.' And with Bettine fully in favour of a swift departure, they went.

'What was eating Rob, I wonder?' Gavin said when they'd gone. 'He seemed a bit on edge.'

'I'm sure I don't know,' Nina replied as if the matter were of little interest. 'Why don't we talk about you instead?'

He was only too willing to oblige, and by the time they'd emptied the wine bottle and the clientele of the Gun and Target were beginning to drift away she was aware that Gavin Shawcross was thirty years old, unmarried and lived in a development of new stone properties in the next village. He was confident and attractive in a bleached sort of way, and she could visualise him having plenty of women friends if the number who'd given him the once-over while they'd been talking was anything to go by.

He might have even created some degree of interest on her own part if she hadn't already met a far more interesting GP than him.

'I'll walk you home,' he offered. 'I can pick my car up on the way back.'

She smiled to take the sting from a refusal and used her father as an excuse. 'No. Thanks just the same. My dad will be on gate duty.'

'I'm not with you.'

'He's ex-army. After eleven-thirty I'm classed as absent without leave,' she told him laughingly, and, leaving him with mouth agape, she strolled off into the night.

As her first week in the practice progressed Nina continued to take stock of those she was working with. So far she'd had little to do with Dr Raju, but on the few occasions when their paths had crossed, kind eyes behind gold-rimmed glasses had met hers benignly and he'd asked politely in his precise English if she was settling in all right.

Each time he'd received her blithe assurance that she was coping he'd gone on his quiet way and she'd been left to show proof of her own assertions.

Gavin's approach to the job was in keeping with his character. He dealt with his patients with confidence and speed, and was always first to be free to carry out his own pursuits.

Bettine Baker was a good doctor. She was clever, cool and critical of almost everything and everyone with the exception of Rob, who gave no inkling of what he thought about her attitude.

On the Friday morning after surgery there was a practice meeting in a room adjoining the computer area in the basement. As Rob took his seat at the head of the table Nina thought that, apart from her family, she had spent more time with this man in the past week than with anyone else in her life.

And where under normal circumstances she would have found it restricting, it hadn't been like that at all, even though he'd been much more aloof after that first memorable day.

In fact, on the second morning, after their meeting outside the Gun and Target the night before, he'd been so cool and impersonal that she'd retreated behind a barrier of her own and it had stayed that way during the days that had followed.

Yet she wouldn't have wanted to have missed it. It mightn't have been war-torn Europe where she was functioning, but it was an exceedingly busy practice that was run in a caring and efficient manner, and as each day came there was something new to learn.

The formidable Ethel Platt had been back to ask belligerently if her test results had come through yet, and at the same time had told Nina, 'I'll be seeing you from now on. That Dr Baker has no patience.'

But the vote of confidence had faltered somewhat when she'd had to tell Ethel that there had still been no news, and the woman had left the surgery with a scowl dark enough to blot out the sun.

However, that was all in the past and now the staff were assembled to discuss the workings of the practice, with the exception of one receptionist left to hold the fort upstairs.

'How long before the decorators are finished?' That was Barbara Walker's first question. 'They seem to have been here for ever.'

Rob nodded. 'Yes, they do, but they aren't finished yet, Barbara. It's all complete down here and they've done the passage between the consulting rooms upstairs, as you can see, but they've all the rest to do yet. Our rooms, the nurses' quarters, and your place. I'm afraid that the smell of paint will be with us for quite some time.'

His eyes went to the girl with the bright green eyes sitting opposite and he smiled. 'Our new trainee can vouch for the fact that there's paint on the premises as some of it came her way on her first visit.'

Nina smiled back and some of the reserve that had been between them during the past few days drained away. As their glances locked, the moment had a promise of its own, but Bettine's voice broke into it.

'I'm sure that we have more important things to discuss than a silly accident. Shall we proceed?'

And proceed they did with the coming week's activities first on the agenda.

With a level look at his fiancée, Rob started off by saying, 'I think that Nina should assist you with the antenatal clinic on Monday, Bettine. It will lighten the workload and give her an insight into the running of our various clinics.'

Dr Baker shrugged narrow shoulders. 'Whatever you say, Rob. Just as long as it *does* lighten the workload.'

Nina eyed her stonily. What did Bettine think she would be doing? Standing there like a dummy? She'd spent some time on a maternity ward in a London hospital and had loved it. If ever she specialised it would be in obstetrics.

Even if Rob had sensed her annoyance, there was no way he was going to take sides and he went on to inform her, 'Gavin takes the asthma clinic on Thursdays and Vikram deals with the psychiatric clinic, which is a fortnightly affair, but for the time being I think it best not to involve you in them.'

'As you're aware, Nina, you'll be spending one day out of each week on one of the courses run by the Department of Postgraduate Medicine and that, along with assisting in the antenatal clinic and your surgeries and call-outs, won't leave much time for anything else.'

'In other words, I won't be getting into mischief,' she said, with a smile for Gavin at the other side of the table.

'Exactly,' Rob agreed drily, as the other man grinned back at her.

That having been sorted, he went on to general practice matters, and some time later a knock on the door preceded the entrance of a small grey-haired man.

As Nina eyed him curiously, Rob said, 'Meet John Burton, the practice accountant, Nina, and unless you're keen to be involved in the financial assessments and cost-benefit analysis for the coming quarter, I think we can let you off the hook.'

She got to her feet obediently, a slender figure, today dressed in beige trousers and a dark green silk blouse that brought out the glints in her russet crop.

'Shall I do some of your calls while you're having your meeting?' she asked rashly, and immediately wished she hadn't, as the thought of doing home visits on her own was terrifying.

Rob thought for a moment. 'Yes, why not? Check with Reception that there's nothing too complicated for you to handle. If you do have any problems, contact me on your mobile.'

'Yes. I'll do that.'

'Then off you go. I'll probably catch you up somewhere along the way.'

As she left, the receptionists and nurses followed suit, leaving the four doctors to discuss their finances with the accountant and elderly Margaret Gray, the practice manager, who held sway over the computer room.

When they surfaced at ground-floor level, Michelle Thomas, the youngest of the receptionists, who'd been left in charge, said, 'You've just missed Ethel Platt, Dr Lombard, enquiring about her test results.'

'Lucky me!' Nina said laughingly, then added on a more serious note, 'I take it they're not back yet?'

The girl shook her head and Nina felt a stirring of anxiety. It was a bit soon for them to have arrived, but Ethel was obviously worried about what they might show. A phone call to the hospital to hurry them along would do no harm, followed by a tactful word from herself.

'Could you chase them up for me, Michelle?' she asked.

As she'd made her way back upstairs from the meeting Nina had thought that it was a relief to get away from Bettine's cold gaze and, even if that hadn't been the case, she would still have been happy to escape from a session of facts and figures that didn't concern her.

If she'd intended to stay in this place, with a possible future partnership, it would have been a different matter, but as that wasn't part of her plans she'd been happy to leave the meeting with all speed.

But as much as she'd been aware that Bettine had been glad to see the back of her and that Rob hadn't been bursting to have her around at that moment, she'd sensed that Gavin would have rather she'd stayed, though for what she felt sure were reasons unconnected with practice matters.

Ever since that first night when they'd chatted at the pub he'd been coming on to her, waylaying her whenever he got the chance and twice suggesting that they get together again socially.

But she wasn't interested. Why, she wasn't quite sure, as he was attractive and articulate in his own way.

Dating him would certainly liven up her life and Eloise would be delighted that she'd found some company nearer her own age. But did she want to be embroiled with one of the partners in the practice before she'd hardly had time to get her breath?

The answer to that was yes, but it was a different member of the team that she had in mind and those sorts of fantasies weren't going to get her anywhere. Not with Rob's fiancée on the scene both workwise and socially, and the man himself proving to be much more remote than her fascinating companion of that first day.

There were half a dozen calls that normally she would be making in Rob's company, and, determined to show him that she could cope, Nina set off purposefully towards the first on the list.

The young housewife who opened the door to her looked dreadful. She was flushed and in the middle of a coughing fit. Unable to get her breath, she beckoned for Nina to enter and when the coughing had subsided she croaked, 'I'm sorry to have called you out, Doctor, but I felt too ill to come to the surgery.'

Nina was already preparing to sound the woman's chest and lungs, and when she'd done so she said, 'Don't worry about it. You did the sensible thing by calling us out. You've got a bad dose of the flu bug that's going around, and you could have passed it on to others in the waiting room if you'd come to the surgery.

'In fact, your condition is bordering on pneumonia. If the antibiotics I'm going to prescribe haven't started to clear your lungs by the end of the next couple of days, send for us again. In the meantime, stay put. Plenty of fluids and go back to bed until you feel better.'

When she got outside Nina took a deep breath. One

down, five to go. The woman's symptoms had been very similar to those of Sara Forrester, the owner of the art gallery, but not quite as severe. Yet they'd been clear enough to convince her that here was another flu victim.

Her next call was to the post office where the proprietor's elderly mother was due for a routine visit to check on various ailments associated with age, but before Nina could make her way there a call came through on her mobile to say that the other doctors were still in conference and asking her to go to the hotel, where a guest was complaining of severe chest pains.

The receptionist at the Royal Venison smiled her relief when she saw her and said, 'The man is in room twenty-five, Doctor. He went for a walk this morning and seemed fine, but when he went up to his room afterwards he started having chest pains and asked us to call a doctor.'

'Right,' Nina said, with what she hoped came over as quiet confidence. 'Show me the way and I'll have a look at him.'

During the first few moments of examination it was clear that all the signs of a heart attack were there—severe pain in the centre of the chest, breathing difficulties, the skin cold and clammy. All very worrying for a man who on the face of it was a healthy-looking, though overweight forty-year-old.

The manager and housekeeper were hovering, and she told them in a low voice, 'I'm going to ring for an ambulance to take the patient into Coronary Care. I suspect a heart attack. He needs prompt treatment.'

Reaching for the bedside phone, she dialled the emergency services and was told that an ambulance would be on its way immediately.

'Keep calm,' she told the man gently. 'Help is on its way. I'm sending you to hospital. I think that you've had a mild heart attack.'

He nodded and said with a gasping sort of groan, 'I thought it might be my ticker, and here I am on a walking holiday. Can't be anything more healthy than that.'

Nina's smile was wry. 'Yes, but what about these?' she said, pointing to an ashtray full of cigarette stubs and an empty wine bottle.

The pain seemed to be lessening and his breathing was more even. He even managed a weak smile. 'You think they're to blame.'

'Let's say that they won't have helped.'

The manager was looking at his watch. 'How long do you think the ambulance will be?' he asked with an anxious glance at the man on the bed.

He doesn't want him to die on the premises, Nina thought. Bad for trade. But it's not food poisoning the fellow's got.

Within minutes the manager's worries were over. The patient was on his way to the main hospital in the area and Nina had accepted the offer of a quick coffee on a terrace beside the strutting peacocks.

She was making haste to down it. If Rob's reluctance to stop for refreshments the other day was anything to go by, it would be frowned upon if he found her here.

But that wasn't going to happen, was it? The call to the hotel had been an emergency. It wasn't on her list. Neither was the stop she intended to make at Ethel Platt's cottage, but she intended calling there nevertheless.

As she checked the woman's address Nina saw that it

was nearer than the post office, so why not call there first?

'They've come at last, have they?' the sour-faced villager said when she saw Nina on the doorstep.

'No. I'm afraid not, Mrs Platt,' Nina informed her with her most winning smile. 'Can I come in for a moment?'

The woman stepped back reluctantly. 'Yes, but I don't see why if you've nothing to tell me.'

As Nina sat down carefully on a horsehair sofa that pricked her legs through the trousers she was wearing, she explained, 'I asked one of the receptionists to ring the hospital before I left the surgery. They said that it will be a couple of days before we get your results, and I thought I'd better let you know as I don't like to think that you're getting stressed because of the waiting.'

'I'm "stressed" all right, if that's supposed to mean the same as "worried sick",' Ethel Platt said shrilly, 'and it's not because I'm afraid of dying. It's what's going to happen to my cats if I pop off that's getting to me.'

'Don't you think you're being a bit premature?' Nina suggested. 'There may be nothing wrong with you—and if there is, it doesn't follow that it will be that serious.'

Ethel wasn't to be consoled. 'It'll happen one day, though, won't it? As long as I know they've got good homes to go to, I'll die happy.'

'How many cats have you got?' Nina asked warily.

'Four. Tiddles, Topsy, Toby and Titmarsh,' she said affectionately, and Nina thought that there was no snappiness about Ethel when she was discussing her cats.

'Well, look, Ethel,' she said with a decisiveness that she knew she was going to regret, 'if it will make you feel any better, I'll have two of your cats in the event of anything ever happening to you.'

Ethel smiled for the first time. 'That's very good of you…Doctor. You've taken a weight off me mind.' Her face sobered again. 'But what about the other two?'

At that moment there was a ring on the doorbell, and when Ethel went to answer it Nina could hear Rob's voice outside. Within seconds he came striding into the small sitting room of the cottage and she could see that he wasn't pleased. But before it had time to register that his expression might have something to do with her, she made matters worse.

'Dr Carslake will have the other two, won't you?' she said with a wheedling smile.

'What will I have?' he asked grimly.

'Mrs Platt is worried about what will happen to her four cats if anything happens to her,' Nina said, oblivious that she was rushing in where angels feared to tread.

'And?' he said through gritted teeth.

'I've promised that I'll have two of them should such a sad thing occur.'

'And?' He didn't sound any happier.

'I thought that you might be willing to have the other two. It would put her mind at rest.'

'It would indeed,' the elderly woman said fervently, and when Rob saw the expression on her face he bit back his overwhelming desire to tell Nina Lombard to mind her own business and stop interfering in his affairs.

He *was* going to do it. Oh, yes, he was going to do it, but not in front of the worried cat owner.

'I think I could manage that, Ethel,' he said, forcing himself to sound agreeable, 'but I'm hoping that the situation won't arise for many years to come. And if it should, are you sure that you'd be happy for your pussy-cats to have to live in an upstairs flat?'

She smiled...for the second time. 'Maybe by then you'll be wed and living in a nice house with little 'uns who'll play with Tiddles, Topsy, Toby and Titmarsh.'

He swallowed hard. 'Yes, maybe that will be the case,' he said stiffly, and indicated that it was time he and Nina were on their way. As they left, Ethel called after them, 'I'll have it put in my will that you folks are going to take my babies.'

'Over my dead body!' Rob snarled when they reached the pavement.

Nina laughed. 'It would be over Ethel's dead body.'

'Very funny! Almost as amusing as the way I've been trying to track you down ever since I left the surgery. How dare you take it upon yourself to start detouring when you're supposed to be looking after the patients?

'Ethel Platt's name wasn't down for a visit today, and where the dickens did you get to after you'd made your first call? Have you been to see old Mrs Armley at the post office yet?'

'No, I haven't,' she told him defiantly.

'And why is that?'

No way was she going to tell him that she'd been called to a suspected heart attack while he was in this mood. Maybe Robert Carslake wasn't so fanciable after all.

'I was going there next.'

'Oh! Well! I suppose I should be thankful for that, then,' he snapped, still angry. 'What do you think this is—a merry-go-round? Where you can float off to where the mood takes you? Visit who you think you will...and on top of that lumber me with the possibility of inheriting two moggies?'

'So you don't like cats?'

'I do, as a matter of fact, but I would prefer to please myself in the matters of pets. Not have some interfering trainee making up my mind for me!'

'Right, well, I'm sorry, then…for everything,' she told him in a voice that was deceptively docile. 'For answering the emergency call that the surgery put through to me regarding a suspected heart attack at the hotel. For trying to allay Ethel Platt's fears and anxiety about her urology tests—just in case you thought I'd called round merely to talk about her pets. And last, but not least, for getting you involved in her last will and testament.'

Rob's face was a study by the time she'd finished, and before he could get a word in she said in the same mild manner, 'Am I not supposed to use my initiative, then?'

'The answer to that is yes, of course you are. And if they'd thought to inform me of the emergency at the hotel before I left the practice I wouldn't have been roaming the streets like a fool, trying to find you.'

'Maybe the message came through after you'd left.'

'Yes, maybe it did. You're just too clever for your own good, aren't you?' he growled, but the heat had gone out of him, and in the next second it was Nina's turn to have the wind taken out of her sails.

'I'm sorry I was so narky,' he said quietly. 'I'd already had my feathers ruffled before I left the surgery.'

'Who by?'

'It doesn't matter. Let's finish the rounds, shall we? And, Nina…'

'Yes?'

There was something in his voice that demanded her full attention. 'I have no regrets about taking you into the practice, you know. You're like a breath of fresh air.'

As her lips parted and the green eyes shone, he spoilt it by saying, 'I think that's how we all see you.'

'Except for Dr Baker. She doesn't see me like that.'

'Ah, yes, Bettine. Maybe it's a good time to change the subject.'

They were on the main street, still on the pavement outside Ethel's house and in full view of passers-by, but she didn't care. He had just told her in an oblique sort of way that he liked her. Probably not as much as she already liked him, but he wasn't averse to her, which was something to be going on with. Carried away by the pleasure of the moment, Nina leaned forward and kissed his cheek.

'Thanks for the vote of confidence, Dr Carslake,' she said softly as her lips lingered against his stubble. 'I'm taking it that the breath of fresh air that you're likening me to is the Stepping Dearsley kind, rather than the carbon monoxide variety?'

'You can bet on that,' he said with laughter in his voice, 'and will you please move your mouth before I do something that I know I will regret?'

The first thing they heard on returning to the surgery were raised voices, and Rob frowned. 'What's going on, Vikram?' he asked Dr Raju.

'I'm not sure,' he replied. 'I think maybe that Bettine said something to Gavin that he objected to, and they ended up in a disagreement.'

'I see.'

Nina noticed that he didn't take it any further. Didn't expect his colleague to tell tales. Rob would sort it out in his own way, no doubt, and she knew instinctively that he would be totally fair. But if he'd wanted to confront them together, he was to be disappointed.

At that moment Bettine flounced out to her car, and before Rob could speak to her she'd gone. When he emerged after confronting Gavin his face was expressionless, and as Nina eyed him questioningly he said abruptly, 'Gavin tells me that it was just a minor tiff that got out of hand.'

'It didn't sound like that to me,' she remarked.

'Save the smart comments, Nina,' he said with sudden weariness. 'The waiting room is full and I'm afraid that I'm going to leave you and the others to cope as I have something to attend to. Once I've dealt with it I intend to have a quiet weekend to take away the feeling of forever being on a tightrope.'

He was about to go through the front door of the practice, but he turned on his heel and said with the vestige of a smile, 'By the way, what were those cats called?'

'Tiddles, Topsy, Toby and Titmarsh.'

'Ugh!' he groaned. 'I can see that we're going to have to keep Ethel Platt in good health.'

With his face set and grim determination in his stride, Rob was walking up the hillside to the biggest house in the area with one purpose in mind.

He had to reach an understanding with Bettine. They couldn't go on as they had been. For one thing he wasn't in love with her, and for another....

Shaking his head, he told himself that this other thing

that was beginning to fill his waking thoughts was just midsummer madness, nothing more.

It was crazy that it was his fiancée's behaviour in the surgery that was proving to be the last straw when there were so many other reasons to call off the engagement, but brawling between partners in the practice wasn't to be tolerated.

He'd played it down to Nina, but it had been a full-scale row, from what he could gather, and Gavin hadn't been to blame.

When he got to the hall she wasn't there. Obviously seeking a diversion, she'd gone elsewhere. Tearing himself away from his website for a moment, her young brother, Miles, told him, 'Bettine has gone riding.'

'And when will she be back?' Rob asked.

'Don't know,' his youthful informant said, his eyes on the screen once more.

'I'll wait,' he told the lad, and settled himself in a seat near the window, deciding that nothing was going to deny him the opportunity of clearing the air *and* his thought processes at one and the same time.

It was two hours later before he heard the clatter of hoofs on the cobbles outside, and when he looked out Rob saw that Bettine wasn't alone. Keith Blackmore, the oldest son of the owner of the biggest farm in the area, was riding beside her.

As he watched, the man dismounted and then went to lift his companion down from her lofty perch. But instead of releasing her once her feet were on the ground, the burly farmer took Bettine into his arms and kissed her.

It didn't last long, but it was long enough for Rob to get a few things into perspective. He couldn't see her reaction as she was obscured by the farmer's broad back, but she didn't push him away—far from it—which had to mean something.

When Keith had gone riding off down the hillside Bettine came into the house with a smug little smile on her face, but the sight of Rob waiting for her in the hall wiped it off.

'Enjoy your ride?' he asked coldly.

'Er…yes… It was lovely up on the tops. How long have you been here?'

'A couple of hours—and long enough to see that you're very chummy with Tom Blackmore's son.'

She shrugged as if what he was saying was of little importance, and the gesture was her undoing.

'It was just a kiss between friends,' she said in a tone that was in keeping with the shrug.

'I see. So it was of no importance? That being so, it will be interesting to see just how important what *I've* come to say is.'

'What is it?' she asked.

'It's over, Bettine,' he said quietly. 'I think that we both know we made a mistake, so let's call it a day, shall we?'

She sank onto the nearest chair and with her head bent was gazing at the carpet without speaking.

'If we call off the engagement I'll look a fool in front of everyone,' she said at last. 'They'll know that you've dumped me.'

'And that's all you care about?' he cried incredulously. 'No sorrow about what might have been? Or thoughts of happier times? Just pique because your pride is going to be hurt?

'I'm going,' he told her. 'Now you'll be able to take

up where you left off with Keith Blackmore. He'll in-
herit the farm one day when the Parkinson's finally takes
his dad, which will make him a much better catch than
a GP who has every penny tied up in a country practice.'

As she started to get to her feet he waved her back
down. 'No need to get up. I'll see myself out.'

When he thought about it afterwards there was no
regret in him. The relationship had been as dead as the
dodo. Had been dead even before he'd met the green-
eyed temptress who'd come to work in the practice.

If Bettine was going to find it difficult to accept that
it was over, that was her problem. As far as he was
concerned, it was a great weight off his mind, and for
the rest of the day he put any thoughts of Nina Lombard
firmly to one side.

CHAPTER FOUR

IF HER mentor had promised himself a restful weekend, with surprisingly no mention of the dark-haired Bettine being part of it, Nina found that leisure wasn't to be her own lot.

Eloise was taken ill during Friday night and, doctor though she was, Nina was just as distressed as the next person to see someone she loved so poorly.

The older woman had seemed to be coping reasonably well with the chemotherapy and on her last hospital visit, which had been just before Nina had come back home to live, tests had shown that there was some improvement, but now it seemed to have all gone haywire.

Unless, Nina thought frantically as she changed the bed sheets for the fourth time and tried to make her stepmother comfortable, there was something else wrong with her.

The symptoms of the flu that was laying half the village low were there, but Eloise was vomiting violently all the time, and the frantic young doctor had seen patients in the very last stages of cancer in that state.

Her father was no use. He kept brewing the strong black tea that he swore by and urging, 'Buck up, old girl. Plenty of fight left in you yet.'

Dared she ring Rob? Nina asked herself as daylight began to filter through the curtains. Last night he'd sounded as if he was going to opt out for forty-eight hours. How would he react if she were to break into the privacy of his weekend?

He's a doctor, for heaven's sake, she told herself desperately. If Eloise dies and you haven't sought more experienced help, you'll never forgive yourself.

You could ring one of the other doctors, the voice of sweet reason reminded her. But she didn't want one of them, did she? She wanted Rob to come to Eloise.

'Yes, who is it?' he said in a voice slurred with sleep when she rang him.

'It's Nina, Rob.'

'Nina!' he exploded. 'For God's sake! Have you seen the time? Even the birds aren't up. What the dickens do you want of me at this hour? I would have thought we'd communicated enough during the past week.'

'Rob!' she protested raggedly. 'Please, let me get a word in. Eloise is really poorly and I don't know what I'm dealing with. I can't tell whether the cancer has escalated or if she's picked up this dreadful flu bug...or even if there's something else wrong.'

There was a moment's silence and then his voice came through again. This time his quiet decisiveness was there. 'Give me time to throw on some clothes and I'll be right with you,' he said and her legs seemed to turn to jelly with relief.

But before she could express her gratitude he was saying to someone other than herself, 'Move over, you lazy creature, while I get out of bed.'

Her heart sank. So he wasn't alone. She was dragging him out of bed and it didn't take much imagination to work out who he was sharing it with.

'Ten minutes, Nina,' he was saying, and with a grateful word of thanks she slowly replaced the receiver.

When she heard his step on the stairs Nina took Eloise's limp hand in hers. 'Dr Carslake is here, darling,' she said.

Her stepmother nodded, too weak to talk, and Nina sent up a silent prayer. Don't let it be the cancer, she begged of the unseen fates. But if it wasn't...what was it that was making Eloise so ill?

Rob's face was grave when he'd finished examining the sick woman. 'I'm going to have you admitted to the oncology unit at the hospital, Eloise,' he said gently. 'I don't think it's the cancer. It's more likely to be the flu bug that's going around, but we can't take any chances. The chemotherapy will have weakened your resistance to infection and, whatever it proves to be that is making you so ill, you're going to need hospital treatment to get you through this.'

For once her father had no irritating platitudes to offer, and as they waited for the ambulance to arrive Nina put her arm around his shoulders. At that moment the upright military stance he was so proud of was missing. His was the bowed back of an old and worried man.

'I'll follow on behind,' Rob said when Eloise had been carefully stretchered into the vehicle and Nina and her father had climbed in beside her.

'Are you sure?' his newest member of staff asked in feeble protest. 'I feel that I've already imposed on you enough.'

The ambulance driver was waiting to close the doors and, without answering her question, Rob said to him, 'You need to get moving. I'll be right behind you.'

It was Saturday afternoon, and the oncology unit had just confirmed that Eloise's cancer was still stable. It was a bad dose of flu which had made her so ill in her weakened state.

'We're keeping Mrs Lombard in until her condition improves,' the consultant told them. 'It's going to take time to get her chest and lungs clear and we need to be at hand in case the vomiting starts again, but you can rest easy that the cancer is still behaving itself.'

As he observed Nina's white face and took in her father's unaccustomed docility, he said to Rob, 'Take these tired people home, Dr Carslake. Mrs Lombard is sleeping. They can come back later.'

When Nina would have refused, Rob took her arm. 'Come on, Nina. You're exhausted. Do as the consultant says.' Without giving her time to argue, he propelled her out into the corridor.

On the drive back she said limply, 'Won't anyone be wondering where you are? I dragged you out of bed at five o'clock this morning. It's ages since you left the flat.'

His eyes were on the road and, without turning his head, he said briefly, 'Don't worry about me. Anyone anxious about my whereabouts will have to persist until they find me.'

Neither of them had actually mentioned a name, yet they both knew who was being discussed. Succumbing to an urge to bring even more gloom into a day that had already had its share, Nina said, 'At least she knew where you were off to at such an hour. I heard you talking.'

This time he did take his eyes off the road momentarily. 'That's right, you did. You heard me talking to Zacky, my Border terrier, who insists on draping himself across me when I'm in bed.'

'So you weren't with…' Her voice trailed away. She was being incredibly nosy and it would serve her right if he told her so.

'Bettine? No, I wasn't with Bettine,' he informed her in clipped tones. Neither will I ever be again, he thought grimly, but as yet Nina wasn't aware that the engagement was over.

'Grateful for your help,' Peter Lombard mumbled when Rob was about to leave, after taking them home. 'Above and beyond the call of duty.'

The two doctors exchanged amused glances and Nina thought gratefully that her father must be rallying if he was back to using army jargon. Better that than the mantle of the geriatric that he'd been wearing ever since Eloise had started to be ill.

'I know I don't need to ask if you'll be going back to the hospital later,' Rob said as she went to the door with him.

'Correct, but I shall insist that Dad stays here. He's had enough for one day.'

He nodded in agreement. 'I'll take you if you like.'

It was a tempting offer. His presence and support would be more than welcome, but this man belonged to someone else and Nina was beginning to rely on him too much.

They hadn't known each other long, although it didn't feel like that. Caution was telling her to slow down. But did she want to be cautious?

She was young, impetuous...and passionate. Certainly not the type to endure the pain and embarrassment of unrequited love, but so far there'd been no sign that the attraction she felt for him was returned.

'Thanks for the offer, but you've done enough,' she told him. 'The Mini will get me there and I won't stay long, unless there's further cause for alarm.'

Perversely, after refusing his offer, she wanted him to persist, but he didn't.

'All right, if that's how you want it,' he said, 'but

remember that I'm only a short distance away if you need me.'

'I won't forget,' she promised, and as he eased himself into the driving seat and prepared to pull off, Nina wished he would take her back to his quiet flat and hold her close...not so much in passion as in comfort.

Nina spent what was left of the weekend between the hospital and the house. Rob rang up on Sunday morning to enquire about Eloise, and when she told him that they'd managed to stop the vomiting and that the antibiotics were beginning to take effect he said, 'So you're coping?'

The answer to that was yes and no. She was dealing with any problems as they came along, giving Eloise all the support that she possibly could and taking her father's idiosyncrasies in her stride, all with commendable calm. Although that was how she would have expected to behave, having fended for herself all the time she'd been at medical school. What wasn't the same was that she felt miserable, lonely and strangely off balance.

There wasn't time to analyse her feelings, which was perhaps as well. Coming to Stepping Dearsley hadn't been a matter of choice. She'd come because she'd been needed, but every time she had an odd moment to herself Nina thought that it had been a mistake as far as her emotions were concerned.

The toughie wasn't as tough as she'd thought. In fact, she was amazed that she could be so vulnerable. Or was it a case of her finding herself hemmed in by a situation that she couldn't cope with?

It was the first time she'd ever got herself in a state over a man, and one belonging to someone else at that, but, she consoled herself, it was early days. As she got to know Rob better, the magic might wear off.

Was there a force at work conspiring to continually bring him into the orbit of his newest member of staff? Rob had asked himself on Saturday evening.

Having nominated himself as Nina's trainer, he had to spend time with her in the practice, but the last thing he'd expected had been her phone call in the summer dawn.

There'd been nothing of the confident young madam about Nina then. Her distress had evoked tenderness in him. She loved the gracious woman who had been the mother figure through her most vulnerable years, and not being able to ease Eloise's pain and discomfort had driven her to ring him.

He hadn't hesitated to go to them, but when the crisis had been sorted out, and he'd returned to the empty flat, Rob had thought bleakly that he had better watch it.

It had never been a good idea for members of the practice to get romantically involved, although he and Bettine had done so. Mistakenly as it had turned out, and now what was happening?

A gutsy young female with beautiful green eyes, long legs and a brain had erupted into his life, and what was she? Part of the practice! For how long he didn't know. Maybe he should encourage her to move on.

Eloise was home and looking ghastly. She'd been in hospital a week and now, with the flu bug behind her, she had a lot of recuperating to do.

'Why don't you both have a holiday?' Nina suggested anxiously. 'Some sun and sea air is what you need. I

think a convalescent home would be the ideal place if
we can find one where Dad can stay, too.'

'I'd like that, my dear,' her stepmother said wistfully.
'I'll ask Peter to sort something out. But what about
you? Are you sure you won't be lonely on your own?
I'm well aware that you're used to a much livelier life
than this.'

Nina smiled. 'Don't worry about me. You're the one
that matters. I was beside myself when you were so ill.'

'Yes, I know you were,' Eloise said softly. 'Rob
Carslake told me when he came to see me.'

'When was that?' she asked in surprise. He'd never
mentioned having been to the hospital after that first
night.

'He came in a couple of times. I'm surprised he didn't
tell you.'

That makes two of us, Nina thought glumly. Maybe
he was afraid that she might have suggested they go
together if she'd known. Because ever since those comforting moments when he'd rushed to her side Rob had
kept her at arm's length, and it hurt...a lot.

Peter and Eloise acted on Nina's suggestion and went to
stay in a convalescent home on the Fylde coast for two
weeks, leaving Nina alone in the big white house at the
end of the village.

The days were taken care of, with not a moment to
spare, but the nights were a void to be got through and
every evening she found herself making her way to the
Gun and Target.

Now, as she skirted the square where the art gallery
was, it was with the knowledge that its owner was back
home after her stay in hospital.

And further along the main street, behind lace curtains, Ethel Platt was content to know that there was nothing seriously wrong with her. The blood in her urine was merely an infection that should clear with a course of antibiotics. Nevertheless, she had still added a codicil to her will.

Gavin was always waiting with drinks at the ready when she got to the busy pub, and even though Nina wasn't interested in anything other than a chat she had to admit that he was good company.

'How did the antenatal clinic go?' he asked on the Friday night after her parents had left for the coast.

'Not too bad for a trainee,' she told him casually.

The previous Monday's antenatal clinic, when she should have assisted Bettine for the first time, hadn't materialised. Rob had told her to give it a miss as he'd known that with Eloise hospitalised Nina would want to spend every possible moment with her, and having the afternoon free had meant extra time together.

But with her stepmother making a slow recovery, she'd been expected to make up for lost time, and had presented herself to Bettine and the mothers-to-be on Monday afternoon with a cool confidence that she'd hoped wouldn't falter.

One of the local midwives had been assisting and the health visitor had been expected some time during the clinic to help with day-to-day problems, healthwise or domestic, in the lives of the women assembled there.

The clinic had been held in the room normally used by the practice nurses, and when Nina had gone in she'd found that all had been in readiness. A plentiful supply of paper sheets had been on hand and the necessary equipment for an antenatal clinic laid out beside them, with dressing forceps, slides, lubricant and vaginal speculums well to the fore.

The midwife gave her a welcoming smile and Bettine greeted her amiably enough, but the temperature dropped somewhat when Rob appeared briefly and asked, 'You all right, Nina? Ready for the fray?'

She flashed him a version of the confident smile she'd been displaying and said, 'Yes. Everything's fine, thanks.' Wishing it was the truth.

Everything wasn't fine. Bearable was a better description. He was still the same pleasant, briskly efficient overseer of her training that he'd been in the beginning, but she sensed that he preferred her in small doses, and because of the structure of the practice it wasn't always possible to limit their contact.

That being so, he was adopting an attitude of cool reserve to keep her at bay and, determined not to let him see how much it rankled, she was doing likewise.

The strange thing was that he was just as aloof with Bettine. There were no displays of affection, and she wondered how solid the engagement was. The other woman's ringless hand might have answered that question, but it never occurred to Nina to look.

There were ten mothers-to-be attending the clinic, all in various stages of pregnancy. Not a bad count for a country village, she supposed, and thought mischievously that maybe in rural areas they had more time for the activities that brought about pregnancy.

She'd noticed that there were quite a few children in the village with hair of a dark reddish gold. They were all from different families and Nina wondered if any of these women would produce a red-haired child.

Perhaps one of the fathers had wanderlust, she thought in wicked amusement, or maybe it was something in the soil!

'Two of the mothers-to-be are new patients,' Bettine explained. 'We'll see them first.'

They took one each and, before asking them to undress, went into all details of their medical histories, paying special attention to any previous obstetric experiences.

It was the second child for the young mother that Nina dealt with and she was apprehensive. 'I had a long and painful labour the first time and ended up having a Caesarean section,' she said worriedly. 'Do you think it will be the same again, Doctor?'

'I can't say until I've examined you,' Nina told her. 'If you have a small pelvis that prevents the baby from being born freely, maybe a Caesarean section will be recommended before you get involved in a long labour.'

'Let's hope so,' the nervous patient said. 'We don't want any more children after this, so not being able to have a natural birth won't bother me.'

Nina nodded understandingly and with a reassuring smile asked the woman to go into the cubicle and undress. When she reappeared, wearing an examination robe, the young doctor examined her internally, checking the pelvic organs and the vagina for proof that the woman was pregnant.

She then did a cervical smear test and followed it by carefully checking the size of the pelvis.

'Your pelvis *is* small,' she told the patient. 'That would have been the cause of your problems last time. We'll keep a close watch on the size of the baby all through the pregnancy and it's possible that as you get to the end we'll have to recommend a Caesarean section. But don't worry now. Plenty of time before we get to that.'

Bettine had been hovering, having dispensed with her

patient far more quickly, and when the woman left she said, 'So you *have* had some experience in antenatal care?'

'Yes,' Nina replied, and waited for what was to come next, but if she'd been expecting a pat on the back it wasn't forthcoming.

For the rest of the women, who were well into their pregnancies, it was a matter of checking blood pressures, taking urine samples and weighing, and for those who were complaining of breathlessness, because of the weight they were carrying, the advice to prop themselves up in bed.

The health visitor arrived halfway through the clinic and saw each patient in turn. When the last one had gone on her way and Bettine had disappeared without comment, the midwife had said, 'How's it gone, Nina?'

'All right...I think,' she replied, 'although I suppose Dr Baker may have thought otherwise.'

'Rest assured that you would have heard about it if she did. Not one to keep her criticisms to herself is Bettine.'

Nina nodded. They were in agreement about that. So why couldn't Rob see it? Maybe he did and treated it as part of her professionalism.

There was no sign of him when she went into the consulting area, but Gavin was in evidence. He and Vikram had been taking the afternoon surgery and now he was off to somewhere more relaxing if his outfit was anything to go by.

'Fancy a game of golf?' he asked, on the point of making a quick departure.

'I couldn't even manage noughts and crosses at the moment,' she told him. 'I never seem to come up for air these days.' Unable to help herself, she added, 'Where's Rob?'

'Gone out on an emergency call.'

'Where to?'

'Don't know. If you're that keen to find out, ask one of the receptionists.'

There was an edge to his voice and she wondered if he guessed that she had leanings in that direction, but he was still pushing his charms when they teamed up at the Gun and Target later.

Tonight was no different, except that it was Friday and an empty weekend loomed ahead after her parents' departure.

'Want to go out somewhere tomorrow?' Gavin was asking.

Nina shook her head. He was pleasant company but she didn't want to be alone with him. She knew instinctively that it wouldn't be a good idea, but a thought occurred to her.

'Why don't I have a party?' she suggested impulsively. 'With Dad and Eloise away I've got the house to myself. You know more people than I do, so spread the word around, will you?'

'Are we talking about the "in" crowd, or a gathering from the practice?' he asked.

Firmly putting to one side thoughts of dark, close-cropped hair, eyes of chestnut brown and a mouth that was unexplored territory as far as she was concerned, she said casually, 'No, leave the practice staff out of it. We see enough of them as it is. Ask some of the crowd from here and anyone else you think might put some sparkle into the event.'

If Rob came so would Bettine and, although their private lives rarely intruded into the practice, to see them together for hours on end was more than she wanted to contemplate.

There was also the possibility that they mightn't want to come even if they were invited, but she decided it was best to take no chances.

As a large assortment of trendy young people began to arrive by car and on foot on Saturday evening, Nina began to feel uneasy.

She wouldn't have thought there had been so many of her own age group in the village and the surrounding areas, but it seemed as if there were, and as they came breezing into her parents' neat home, most of them with the token bottle, she couldn't believe that she'd given Gavin a free hand with the invitations.

Nina had provided drinks and tasty nibbles. She'd also made a huge pile of sandwiches, but as people continued to arrive she had a sinking feeling that coping with this lot was going to be like the feeding of the five thousand in biblical times.

Luckily, it was a warm night so the gardens would be occupied just as much as the house, with taped music equally as clear outside as in.

'So!' Gavin said with a smug smile when he arrived. 'I've done as you asked.'

'What?' she snapped. 'Invited the whole of Cheshire? I meant a couple of dozen, not droves of this size. I'll have to make some more sandwiches and heaven knows if we'll have enough to drink.'

'Don't panic,' he said easily. 'If we run out I'll go and get some more and I'll help you with the butties.'

His calmness had the desired effect and she began to unwind, giving her mind to playing the hostess in a long black dress that clung to her slender curves like a second skin.

However, as the night progressed and still guests continued to turn up, the atmosphere of good humour began to change and a quarrelsome note crept in amongst some of them.

A vase that Eloise was fond of had been broken and the crush on the stairs had split one of the polished wooden spindles of the banister.

Nina was beginning to get anxious again. Eloise wouldn't bother too much about the vase but her father would be furious when he saw the staircase.

'That's it, folks,' she called. 'The party's over.'

Gavin was at her elbow. 'It's not twelve o'clock yet,' he said in a scandalised whisper. 'They'll be expecting it to go on for hours.'

'They're in for a disappointment, then, aren't they?' she snarled. 'Your friends are wrecking the place.'

He looked uncomfortable. 'They're not exactly my friends, although I do know some of them. I put a notice up outside the Gun and Target telling anyone who was interested to come along.'

'So you don't know half of them!'

'Afraid not, but you did tell me to spread the word.'

'Not to all corners of the globe! And whether they like it or not, the party's over. You brought them here— you tell them!'

But either they couldn't hear him above noise or if they did they chose to ignore him, as no one took the least bit of notice.

Nina was becoming desperate. Another ornament had been broken and wine had been spilt on the carpet. She must have been insane to have come up with an idea such as this, and she had no idea what she was going to do about it as she was outnumbered.

Having failed to make himself heard, Gavin had given up on it and was dancing out on the terrace with a dark-haired girl wearing black lipstick.

Nina watched them in silent anguish. She had bitten off more than she could chew and knew it. The party would go on all night. By morning the house would be wrecked, and that might be the least of the catastrophes as swaying couples were drifting off upstairs and into the shrubbery amidst ribald comments.

A skinhead in designer clothes with a gold ring in each ear came along at that moment and draped a muscular arm across her shoulders. When she moved away he pulled her back and said with a leer, 'Don't go rushing off, Dr Lombard. I've got a complaint that I want to ask you about.'

She glared at him. 'Really? Then you'd better make an appointment at the surgery.'

His grip on her wrist tightened and he began to pull her towards the bushes. 'We'll talk about it now,' he said drunkenly.

It was Saturday night and it felt strange for it to be free of Bettine's presence, but free it was and Rob had no complaints about that.

So far he'd told no one about the broken engagement and neither had she, which wasn't surprising when he thought about her remarks at the time.

There'd been a couple of comments at the practice about the missing ring but she'd fobbed them off with the excuse that a stone was loose.

As he picked up Zacky's lead and prepared to take the Border terrier for his nightly walk his smile was wry.

It was incredible that his life had been turned upside down in so short a time...and that his footsteps should automatically turn in the direction of the Lombard residence.

And if his subconscious hadn't propelled him towards the house in question, the noise coming from there would have made him curious enough to walk that way.

His eyes widened at the sight of all the cars outside and the light from the windows of every room beaming out across the lawns and flower-beds. Music was blaring out and there was loud laughter and shouting coming from all parts of the house.

He hesitated, debating whether he should make his presence known in case... In case what? The tone of the party needed quietening down? Or to issue a word of warning to the young hostess who needed her head read?

From the sight and sound of it, Rob guessed that there must be at least sixty people there. His jaw tightened. It looked as if the city girl was determined to liven up the countryside.

But if she was that starved of the bright lights, why, for goodness' sake, hadn't she gone there tonight? There'd been nothing to stop her. Her father and Eloise were away and Nina had transport. She was turning his beloved village into a venue for lager louts!

As his anger mounted he saw her in the garden, standing in a pool of light beneath one of the windows. A fellow with a shaved head was beside her and as he watched, Rob saw him grasp her arm and start to drag her off into the shrubbery.

That was enough to have him invading the rowdy gathering. As he sprinted up the drive he caught a glimpse of Gavin's astonished face, which did nothing to reduce his rage. But before he tore a strip off his junior partner he had to get to Nina.

As he reached the bushes she came staggering out, her hair tangled and a scratch on her cheek, while from behind her he could hear a howl of pain.

When she saw him she burst into tears and ran straight into his arms. If the circumstances had been different Rob would have made the most of the moment, but all he could think of was that if she'd organised this disruptive gathering she should have been prepared for this sort of thing to happen. That he couldn't bear the thought of anyone else touching her was a side issue.

He put her away from him with an abrupt movement and moved towards the shrubbery, determined that, if nothing else, he was going to send the lout on his way, but before he could do so the bushes parted and the youth in question came limping out sheepishly.

'Did he harm you?' Rob grated through clenched teeth.

Nina managed a smile through her tears. 'No. He was the one who came off worst.'

'But he could have done!' he persisted as the culprit hobbled off. He looked around him grimly. 'It's insane to invite this many to a party unless you're sure you can keep it under control. I see that Gavin's here, but he wasn't much use to you just then, was he?'

'No,' she mumbled.

She'd been so thankful to see Rob standing there when she'd lurched out of the bushes, but it was clear that the feeling was one-sided. He was looking at her with cold, dark eyes and if she could have blotted out the last few hours she would have done.

'I'm going to get rid of this lot,' he said grimly.

She nodded wretchedly. 'Yes, please.'

'So you do realise that this sort of thing can soon get out of hand?'

'It wasn't meant to be like this, Rob.'

She wasn't going to tell him that Gavin was partly to blame because the main fault was hers. She'd not put a limit on the number he'd been allowed to invite, but she was desperate that Rob shouldn't think too badly of her.

'Stay there while I clear the place!' he commanded, 'and that partner of mine can give me a lift. I shall have something to say to him on Monday.'

'But I'm going to get my telling-off tonight?' she said with an attempt at a smile.

'How did you guess? What you do in your own time is none of my business, but allowing your parents' home to be abused and putting your own safety at risk are the actions of someone who needs straightening out, as I see it.'

'And you're the one to do it?'

'If no one else is around...yes.'

CHAPTER FIVE

THERE was peace. The invaders had gone, some reluctantly, others good-naturedly. But the main thing was that they'd gone.

As Nina looked at the chaos they'd left behind she groaned. Cans, cigarette ends and half-eaten sandwiches were scattered around in abundance. Thank goodness her father and Eloise weren't due home until the following weekend, she thought as she stood amongst the debris.

If they hadn't wanted to take any notice of Gavin and herself, the presence of Dr Carslake, with a face like thunder and a voice to match, had done the trick.

Gavin would have departed with them but Rob had other ideas. 'Don't go slinking off,' he told him. 'You can assist with the cleaning up.'

When his young partner opened his mouth to protest he snapped, 'Save your breath, Gavin. I don't know what part you had in this affair, but I'm damn sure that Nina didn't know all those people from the short time she's been here. They were your friends, weren't they?'

'Some of them, yes,' Gavin admitted reluctantly. 'But she did tell me to pass the word around. There was no mention of limiting numbers.'

'The pair of you are totally irresponsible. It's a wonder that the police haven't been round to see what the racket was.' Rob pointed to the sink. 'After you've collected all the rubbish that's lying around you can start washing some glasses, and after that—'

'Steady on, Rob!' the bleached-haired charmer protested. 'I need my beauty sleep.'

'Huh! You wouldn't have been worrying about that if the party had been still in full swing,' he said relentlessly. 'There's an apron behind the door. I suggest you put it on.'

'And what are you going to do while I'm slaving over the sink?'

'I'm going to find Nina.'

He found her staring gloomily at the broken banister, but her expression changed to surprise when she saw the bowl in his hand.

'Sit down,' he commanded, and as she sank onto the nearest step he produced lint and a tube of antiseptic cream.

'I foraged for these in the kitchen. I hope you don't mind,' he said levelly.

'No, of course not,' she said warily. 'What are you intending to do with them?'

He rolled his eyes heavenwards. 'Well, I'm not proposing to use them to repair the staircase, if that's what you're thinking. I'm going to bathe your face, of course. That's a nasty cut.'

Nina touched her face absently where the branches had caught it. 'I thought it was stinging but my mind has been on other things, I'm afraid. My dad will be so angry when he sees the broken banister.'

'You don't deserve it, but I'll ask the joiner who's working on the alterations at the surgery to come round and repair it on Monday,' Rob said flatly.

'Oh! Thanks, Rob!' she breathed. 'I know I don't deserve it, but thanks.'

'I'm not doing it for you,' he told her in the same cold

tones. 'I'm thinking of your father and Eloise. And now, if you'll keep quite still, I'll attend to your face.'

His touch was more gentle than his voice had been, and as he crouched down beside her and began to bathe the gash on her cheek Nina was conscious of his face close to hers.

She wanted to reach up and brush his lips with her fingers, trail them around the dark eyes that were so intent on what he was doing, caress his strong neck... Desire was rising in her like a floodtide.

'Stop it, Nina!' he commanded harshly.

'What do you mean?'

'I mean that I know what you're thinking.'

'And what's that?'

'That everything and everyone is yours for the taking when the mood strikes you.'

She slumped back against the wooden stair, feeling as if she'd just been struck in the chest. So that was what he thought of her. Spoilt! Selfish! Greedy! Couldn't he see that she was in love with him? That the way she felt about him wasn't a here-today-and-gone-tomorrow sort of thing?

As he watched her mouth droop in dismay and the beautiful green eyes cloud over, Rob's anger drained away. Tonight Nina Lombard had been the victim of her own impetuosity, which was a fact that would be brought home to her when she started the mammoth clean-up that would have to be done.

But as his eyes dwelt on her downcast face, Rob was having to admit to himself that his anger had come not from the stupid thing she'd done but because she'd put herself at risk at the hands of some local stud. Adding insult to injury, she'd invited that preening oaf, Gavin, to the party, but hadn't contemplated asking himself.

He'd come in useful for the clearing-out process and that was all.

Then in his pique he'd just told her in no uncertain terms that he wasn't available for whatever she might have in mind. Since when had his thought processes been in such a mess?

She was still crouching on the step, and as the clatter of pots continued to come from the kitchen Rob reached out to help her up.

When their hands met the effect of the touch was electrical. The only time they'd ever been in physical contact before had been when she'd planted a butterfly kiss on his cheek. This was hardly a lovers' embrace, but it was enough to make his blood run warm and his pulses race.

As she came upright to stand hesitantly before him, everything else but the two of them ceased to exist. Was this what he'd been missing? he asked himself, and realised that he'd never know if he didn't take this opportunity being offered.

He heard Nina gasp as his mouth took possession of hers and then she was pressing herself to him and kissing him back as if the world were about to end.

So that's how the land lies, Gavin thought as he stood in the hallway below with a glass cloth in his hands and soapy splashes down the front of his smart waistcoat.

Washing pots wasn't his scene. At home everything went into the dishwasher, and it was that fact which had brought him out of the kitchen to protest that he'd had enough and was going home.

However, he'd been stopped in his tracks at the sight of Nina and Rob locked in each other's arms.

So that was why he was making no progress with her, he thought wryly as he let himself quietly out of the back door. The party girl had other fish to fry.

Totally engrossed in each other, they didn't hear him go. But if Gavin hadn't been prepared to butt into the moment, common sense and logic had no such scruples.

Even as he held Nina close Rob's mind was beginning to function again, and the messages that were issuing forth were telling him that she wasn't the only one who'd been stupid on this mellow summer night.

He'd already made it clear to Bettine that they had no future together. So what was he thinking of? He was the one who frowned on relationships within the practice and yet here he was, ready and willing to make a fool of himself with another of its doctors. This time its youngest one.

He put her away from him gently. 'I must be insane, Nina. It has to stop.'

'Yes, of course,' she agreed forlornly. 'For a crazy moment I forgot that you belong to someone else.'

It was hardly the right moment but Rob knew that he couldn't go on keeping the truth from her.

'I don't belong to anyone else, Nina,' he said quietly. 'That's not the reason I'm holding back. I've broken off my engagement. Bettine is out of my life permanently.'

Nina could feel her jaw sagging. 'So why can't we—?'

'Because for one thing I've just had a disastrous relationship with a practice member and I don't want another.'

'So you think that being involved with me would be just as bad as Bettine?' she cried dismally.

'No. I don't. What I meant was that I don't think it would be wise to have another relationship with anyone in the practice, be it good, bad or indifferent.'

'I see,' she said flatly, and, trailing her hand along the banister, she began to mount the stairs.

'Aren't you going to lock up?' he called after her.

She shrugged slim shoulders.

'Someone had better,' he insisted, 'in case the shaven-headed predator turns up again.'

Nina turned and looked down on him from the top step. 'At least I would know what's in *his* mind.'

'Now you're being ridiculous,' Rob told her.

Locking the doors behind him, he went to find Zacky, who was waiting patiently for him on the terrace.

'I hear that you've some repair work that needs doing,' the joiner said on Monday morning. 'Had a bit of a hectic night, did you? You'd better let me have a key. I'll go and see what the damage is.'

Nina sighed as she handed it over. Hearing her, Barbara, who was on Reception, said sympathetically, 'Parties can soon get out of hand.'

So it looked as if everyone at the practice knew about Saturday's fiasco, Nina thought dismally. She hoped that when he'd told them Rob had missed out the last bit.

But, then, he would have, wouldn't he? He wasn't going to admit to the rest of them that he'd had a quick flirt with someone as irresponsible as her.

He was in his consulting room, and when she went in to see if he had any instructions for her before surgery started Nina said coldly, 'Thanks for telling everyone about Saturday.'

'What?' he said with equal chilliness.

'They all appear to know about Saturday night.'

If he'd been angry then, it was nothing compared to now. 'Really?' he snapped. 'Well, they haven't heard it from me. Am I likely to go around broadcasting that I'm the village idiot? You're forgetting that I wasn't the only member of this practice who was there.'

Gavin! Of course! Her face flamed. But Rob wasn't prepared to wait for an apology.

'We have a waiting room full of patients out there, so shall we do what we're paid to do?'

'Yes,' she said meekly, and slunk into her own little sanctum.

The first patient to present himself to her was Spanish. He'd married a local girl and was desperately missing his homeland, so much so that he couldn't eat, sleep or hold down a job.

Slim, dark and extremely handsome, he told her jerkily, 'I am lost away from my country. I shake all the time.'

His eyes were wild. His hands were gesturing all the time he was speaking. One wrong word would send this one over the edge, she thought.

'If it distresses you so much, can you not persuade your wife to live in your country, instead of you having to get accustomed to life over here?' she asked carefully.

He jumped to his feet and, raking his hair with shaking hands, he cried, 'No! She has been there. Has been to the hotel that I help my father to run…but she does not like it.'

It was a clash of cultures, she thought, and the proud Spaniard wasn't coping one little bit. In fact, if he didn't get a grip on himself he was going to be really ill.

'I'm going to prescribe some tablets for you to take,' she said as clearly and concisely as she could. 'Your life has changed dramatically and you aren't coping. Come back to see me in a month if you don't feel any better. You understand? And if you do have to make another appointment, I suggest that you ask your wife to come along.'

He nodded and, holding the prescription for antidepressants in his hand, left the room dejectedly.

She would like to see the girl who'd enticed the homesick Spaniard from his native land, she thought when he'd gone. His English wife must have some very persuasive qualities, but it was going to be touch and go whether he stayed, persuasive or not.

He was followed by a dark-haired, ten-year-old boy with an entrancing smile, who'd been brought in by his mother. It appeared that Jonathan had been stung twice over the weekend by wasps from a nest in the garden.

There was swelling of his face and neck, and his parents had thought it best he see a doctor, even though the boy himself seemed to be in only minor discomfort.

The time for any dangerous complications had passed, and when the mother assured her that there had never been any allergic reaction to stings in the past, it was prescription time again. This time for antihistamine cream.

'So you're the new doctor, are you?' said an old man, leaning heavily on two sticks as he came hobbling in. 'You don't look old enough to be treating the likes of me.'

'I'm a trainee' she told him, 'and I'm older than you might think.'

'Is that so?' he wheezed as he flopped down onto the chair at the other side of the desk. 'And is that supposed to make me feel confident that you can sort me out?'

'I can't guarantee it,' she told him with a smile, 'but I'll do my best. And if I can't, Dr Carslake is next door.'

'Was, you mean. He's the one I usually see, but he's gone. The receptionist said he had some urgent business to attend to, so they've shuffled me in here.'

'Right, so what can I do for you, Mr Wood?' she

asked, digesting the information that Rob had already departed, which must mean that he wasn't taking her on house calls with him today. He really must be sticking to what he'd said on Saturday night...

She'd thought she'd seen paradise beckoning when he'd bathed her face and then taken her in his arms, but she'd been wrong.

She'd been kissed before, lots of times, but by younger men and in a casual manner. With Rob it had been so different...in more ways than one.

To begin with, most men couldn't get enough of her when it came to a bit of light-hearted canoodling, but not him. He'd no sooner turned her into a quivering jelly than he was finding reasons to put a stop to the passion that had flared between them after the party.

And ever since then she'd been trying to come to terms with what he'd said. It should have been one of the happiest moments of her life, being told that his engagement was off, but he'd no sooner said it than he'd been telling her it would make no difference.

'So are you going to be standing there dreaming all day, or what?' the old man growled.

Nina dredged up a smile. 'No, of course not. And I did ask you what the problem was, Mr Wood.'

'Aye, well, now I'm going to tell you. I keep coughin' up blood.'

'I see.'

She wasn't dreaming now. It was the young doctor, keen and intelligent, who was standing in her shoes, alert to all the various possibilities, some of them serious.

'There are various reasons why a person coughs up blood,' she told him. 'It's usually caused by the rupture of blood vessels in the lungs or throat, but there has to be a cause. I want some sputum from you and I need to listen to your chest. Will you unbutton your shirt, please?'

When she'd finished he observed her with watery blue eyes. 'Well? Have I got galloping consumption?'

'You've got a chest that's anything but clear,' she told him, ignoring the joke about tuberculosis as he might have been nearer to the truth than he knew.

'I'm going to arrange for a chest X-ray and we'll take it from there.'

'How soon?'

'As soon as I possibly can. Are you on the phone at home?'

'Yes.'

'I'll get one of the receptionists to ring you when I've arranged an appointment. And, Mr Wood, don't worry. We'll sort you out, one way or another.'

'Kill or cure, you mean?' he asked with a dry chuckle as he got slowly to his feet.

Two things became clear as Nina surfaced from morning surgery, the first being that Gavin was doing his best to avoid her and the second that Bettine hadn't put in an appearance.

The first she could deal with. The second wasn't her affair...or was it?

'Thanks for spreading the details of Saturday night's disaster around the practice,' she told Gavin when she cornered him outside in the parking area. 'Especially as you were partly to blame.'

That brought a scowl to his handsome face. 'You should be thankful that I didn't fill in the folks about *all* that happened,' he said snappily.

Her heart skipped a beat. 'Meaning?'

'That you and Rob were having a party of your own when I went looking for you.'

She rallied. 'What you saw was me, very drunk, pushing my luck.'

'It didn't look like that to me.'

'Obviously you didn't stay long enough. That was all it was.'

'So you and he aren't...?'

'Of course not. You've heard of Saturday night fever, haven't you?' Followed by Sunday morning doldrums, she could have added.

But *she* was the only one who knew just how miserable she'd been the morning after as she'd scrubbed at the wine stains and tried to mend the ornaments with superglue, while telling herself that her own after-effects of the party weren't going to be so easy to cope with.

With Bettine missing, and the women on Reception confirming that Rob had indeed gone out on some urgent matter, Nina went to seek out Dr Raju to ask what she should do about the senior partner's visits to patients.

'I've agreed to do all the calls today,' he told her, 'as Dr Carslake felt that in Dr Baker's absence you would need to be free for this afternoon's antenatal clinic.'

'So I'm taking it on my own?'

'With the help of a midwife, yes. Will that be a problem?'

'Er, no. I don't think so.'

His twinkly smile flashed out. 'I'm sure it won't. It's all experience, my dear.'

She wasn't going to argue about that! But unsatisfied curiosity was taking precedence over the prospect of being in charge of the clinic.

Is Dr Baker ill...on holiday...or what?' she asked casually.

'She isn't well, I'm afraid. Her brother rang earlier to say that she'd suffered some sort of gastric attack. Needless to say, Dr Carslake went to her immediately.'

'Of course,' she murmured.

So the urgent business for which he'd left his patients had been to treat his ex-fiancée's stomach bug! Was there still some chemistry there? He'd left with such speed that someone or something must be pulling his strings.

'Where does she live?'

It was strange that she'd never thought to ask, but she wasn't interested in Bettine Baker, was she?

'Bettine and her young brother live at the old hall up on the hillside there,' Dr Raju informed her. 'The family have lived there for generations and now there are just the two of them left.'

After their brief, angry exchange of words, Rob had sat gazing sombrely into space. Nina had thought he'd told the staff about Saturday night. As if he would! It was the last thing he would think of doing.

For one thing, he didn't want anyone to know he'd been at the Lombard house, and for another, tittle-tattle wasn't his style. The obvious culprit was Gavin, but she'd immediately thought that it had been himself who'd been responsible.

He knew that Nina was hurt at what he'd said, and the way he'd broken up their special moment on the stairs, but surely she must see that they'd only known each other for a very short time and that he was head of the practice.

As he had reached out to buzz for his first patient to present themselves, the phone rang. It was Miles, ringing to say that Bettine wouldn't be available for practice duties.

'What reason does she give?' Rob had asked. As if he didn't know! It would be her way of showing him that he wasn't having it all his own way.

'It's that sickness thing that women have when they're pregnant,' the lad had said vaguely, and Rob had nearly fallen out of his chair.

'I'm coming over,' he'd told him, already on his feet and asking himself whatever had made him think that his troubles were over from that quarter. He should have known better.

If the previous week's antenatal clinic had gone smoothly, it wasn't working out that way today. The midwife assisting this time was younger than Nina and less experienced, so if the young doctor had wanted to shine, the opportunity was there.

But she'd never felt more lacking in sparkle. Rob had returned from his visit to Bettine's place with a face like granite, and after a brief word with Vikram had gone up to the flat.

There hadn't been a smile or even a look in her direction, and if she'd had the nerve Nina would have followed him up there and told him that if that was what she had to endure after just one kiss she'd stay well away from him in future.

But she had a feeling that wouldn't be necessary. That, apart from their work in the practice, she would be lucky if he looked the side she was on in the days to come.

An expectant mother who hadn't been at the previous week's clinic had turned up with symptoms that immediately suggested trouble—headache, excessive thirst, frequent passing of urine and general tiredness, amongst other things.

Nina saw from her notes that the patient was due for the routine screening for gestational diabetes the following week, but with the discomforts she was complaining of Nina felt it was necessary to speed up the process.

'I'm sending you to hospital,' she told her.

'Why?' the woman asked anxiously. 'Is something wrong?'

'You're due to be tested for diabetes next week, but I want you to have it done sooner. Just to be on the safe side.'

Panic was setting in. 'You mean that I might have to have insulin?'

'It's possible, but if there's a problem lots of pregnant women keep the diabetes in check with a special diet. If insulin is required it will be only during the pregnancy. Once the baby is delivered the diabetes should disappear.'

'What will they do when I get there?'

'Nothing very horrible,' Nina said with a reassuring smile. 'They'll give you a dose of glucola and then an hour later test your blood-sugar levels. If they're too high they'll do a three-hour glucose tolerance test and go on from there. I'll keep my fingers crossed and hope that when I see you next week it will have been sorted out.'

'That makes two of us,' the young mother-to-be said with feeling.

The midwife had been hovering. 'I've tested the blood pressure of all those present,' she said nervously, 'and two of them are showing an increase on last week's readings. Would you like to check me out, Doctor?'

Nina nodded.

Come back, Bettine, all is forgiven, she thought wryly as another of the expectant mothers dashed into the toilet to vomit.

One of the patients with raised blood pressure, which had been a major problem during her first pregnancy, had been sent to hospital all weepy and apprehensive at the thought of being admitted.

The other, who was due to move to another area in the next few days, and whose pressure was only slightly up, had been warned to have regular checks the moment she was settled in her new home.

By the time that had been accomplished and the rest of them had thankfully been declared healthy, Nina was beginning to feel that, if nothing else, she had earned her crust.

Rob had come down from the flat by the time she got back to the reception area. He was still looking grim, but not as forbidding as before. When he asked how the clinic had gone and had been told wearily that, apart from suspected diabetes, high blood pressure and a variety of minor ills, it had been all right, he surprised her by saying, 'Gavin will take your surgery tonight. You might as well get off home. The joiner has just come back from your place and he says that it's fixed.'

Her expression lightened. 'Thank goodness for that. If Dad had seen it I'd have been up before a court-martial and, no doubt, shot at dawn. I've still got to confess my sins to Eloise but she's a lot more tolerant than he is.'

At that moment they were alone in the passage outside the consulting rooms and she couldn't resist asking, 'How's Bettine? I believe you were called out to her this morning. I hope that it wasn't anything serious.'

'It all depends on how you look at it,' he said tonelessly. 'She's pregnant.'

As Nina felt her jaw go slack he gave a mirthless laugh. 'End of discussion, wouldn't you say?'

It was, whether Nina wanted it to be or not. Rob was turning towards the door of his room and as it closed behind him she groped her way towards her own small piece of territory.

CHAPTER SIX

THE course arranged by the Department of Postgraduate Medicine to provide prospective GPs with further training on a day-release basis was scheduled for the next day, and there was relief inside Nina as she drove towards the city on Tuesday morning.

She needed time away from the village to think. If everything had been going too fast between Rob and herself since she'd joined the practice, it had been brought to an abrupt halt the moment he'd told her that Bettine was pregnant.

Would they marry now? she'd wondered in the quiet hours of the night. It had to be on the cards. Although it didn't always mean that one event followed the other these days. It used to be the other way about, that the wedding came first, not the baby, and deep down Nina knew that was how she would want it to be for herself.

From what she'd seen of Rob, she'd imagined that he would have had similar feelings, but it didn't appear to be so. Yet he and Bettine were both doctors. For heaven's sake! If anybody knew about the birds and the bees, they should.

So shattered had she been at the news that the excellent repair to the staircase had almost gone unnoticed. She'd given it a cursory glance and then rushed past to throw herself dejectedly on to the bed.

The only bright moment in the evening that followed had been a phone call from Eloise to say that she was feeling much better, which had made Nina's heart lift.

She'd told Eloise about the ornaments being broken, and her stepmother had said characteristically, 'Don't worry, darling. It's unfortunate, but I'm pleased to know that you weren't sitting around moping. With what is going on in my life at the present, a few pieces of coloured glass are the last things I'm going to fret about.'

Nina had wanted to tell her that if she hadn't been moping then, she was now, but that was something else Eloise shouldn't have to worry about—her stepdaughter's flights of fancy. As that was all her expectations with regard to Rob and herself had been.

When she reached the city limits the noise of the traffic was deafening, to such an extent that she was amazed. Being in it every day in the past, she'd scarcely noticed it, but in the last few weeks she'd got used to the quieter, more spacious countryside, hadn't she?

Was that why the adrenaline wasn't flowing faster? Or was it the gloom that had settled on her the previous day that was spoiling the pleasure of being back in her natural habitat?

It might not be London, but it was a big and bustling place, and as Nina looked around for a parking spot she told herself firmly that the sooner she was away from the countryside the better.

But Eloise came first. She would be prepared to vegetate on a desert island, let alone in a pretty country village, rather than that her stepmother should need her and she wasn't there.

They were a pleasant enough crowd on the course. Most of them were of a similar age to herself with a few older graduates amongst them. She was amused to find that the general feeling was of relief to be away for a few hours from the busy practices where they were employed.

Not for the same reason as herself, though. She could cope with the job. It was her gullibility that was the problem. Letting herself get into a state of frustrated longing over a man. Who was about to father a child. That, in her book, made him as out of reach as the sun in the sky. A diamond ring on the finger was one thing. A foetus in the womb another.

As she slid into a seat behind one of the desks in the lecture hall she thought with grim humour that maybe Bettine would be one of her patients at the clinic next week, sitting meekly amongst the other mothers-to-be.

It wasn't likely, though, was it? That one knew enough to treat herself, although on the face of it she wasn't all that well informed about contraception, unless getting pregnant had been deliberate. And meek? Not the confident Dr Baker.

For the rest of the day she worked, looking, listening and learning, with the loose ends of her life temporarily receding.

When a group of her fellow trainees asked her to join them at one of the city's café bars in the early evening she accepted without hesitation, telling herself that this was what she was short of—city life.

It was like it had always been. She was the liveliest one in the party until it was time to say goodbye until the following week and point her red Mini towards rural life once more. It was then that her bounce deserted her.

The hours had gone quickly and it was close on midnight when she turned into the drive of her parents' house. When she got out of the car the stillness of the night was all around her and Nina felt tears prick.

Life and soul of the party she might have been in the crowded bar, but it was in this place that her heart was.

As she was putting her key in the lock Rob's voice

spoke from nearby, and as she swung round, startled, she saw the outline of him in the shadowed garden.

He was standing beside a rustic bench, and as she began to walk towards him he said, 'This seat isn't the most comfortable thing I've ever sat on. I was beginning to think if you didn't come soon I'd be getting saddle-sore.'

'What are you doing here at this time of night?' Nina breathed. 'Not checking up on me again, are you?'

She saw him shake his head in the dim light. 'Not exactly. When I was out walking Zacky earlier I saw that the house was in darkness, but I managed to work out for myself that you'd been lured by the city lights and had stayed on. Correct?'

'Yes,' she said flatly. 'Except that it all turned out to be something of a damp squib.'

She was getting accustomed to the gloom and could see his face more clearly now. He looked puzzled. 'I'm not with you.'

'It was noisy and busy and…I found myself missing this place.'

Rob laughed. 'Well! I never thought I'd live to see the day when you had fond thoughts of… What was it you called it—this "rural backwater"?'

That was before I'd met you, she wanted to cry, but the time for that was past.

Instead, she said casually, 'Maybe I've changed my mind, but getting back to what I asked you. If you weren't checking up on me, what are you doing here? Shouldn't you be with your pregnant ex-partner?'

'Er…no,' he said calmly.

'No?' she echoed angrily. 'You have a strange set of values. Surely Bettine's pregnancy changes everything.

The engagement might be off, but the aftermath of it is there.'

If Nina had expected that to bring forth a positive response, she was disappointed.

'Could I get a word in, please?' he said equably. When she nodded grimly, he went on, 'As far as I'm concerned it's over.'

'*What?*' she cried. 'You're despicable. You've dumped her!'

'I called it off before I knew Bettine was pregnant,' he reminded her in the same mild tone.

'Pull the other leg,' she said mockingly.

'I'm not in the habit of lying, Nina,' he retaliated, and now his voice wasn't so calm. 'At the time I was surprised at the way she took the news. She wasn't upset that I wanted to finish it. Bettine was more put out at the thought of being pitied or made to look a fool. In other words, it was her pride that she was bothered about.'

'Especially with a child inside her,' Nina said drily. 'So what are you going to do?'

'Nothing.'

'You can't just do nothing,' she protested. 'You've got to face up to your responsibilities.'

Nina couldn't believe it was happening. She was telling him what he had to do. Criticising *his* motives! Lecturing *him* on how to behave!

Rob's face was sombre in the darkness.

'The reason I'm about to do nothing is because I'm not involved. I'm not the father.'

She was rocking on her feet, holding onto one of the porch supports as if her life depended on it.

'How can you be sure?' she gasped.

'How do you think? Because I've never slept with her.

Prude though I might appear to be, I do have values, and if after that confession you still think them to be strange, too bad. It's clear that my ex-fiancée must have seen them in that light, and she dealt with what she saw as my shortcomings by sleeping with a local farmer.'

As she goggled at him, speechless, he went on, 'You remember the first visit I took you on? The old man with Parkinson's disease? Bettine has been sleeping with his son. He's the father of her child.'

'Why are you telling me all this?' Nina asked into the silence that had fallen when he'd finished speaking.

Hope was leaping inside her, the future a pathway they would walk together.

'I wanted you to know exactly what the situation is. In other words, I want no more loose ends in my life. Bettine's deceit has left a very nasty taste in my mouth. I'm the one who's been made to look a fool, not her, but, unlike my ex-fiancée, I can take it.

'I came here to tell you that I don't want you getting any wrong ideas about me after Saturday night. It was a one-off. As I said to you before, I've already had a bad relationship with one member of the practice and don't want another.'

'And as I remarked on that occasion, you're tarring me with the same brush as Bettine,' she choked.

'I didn't mean it like that.'

'No? That's what it sounded like. Well, you've no need to worry about me making a nuisance of myself from now on. The moment I can be sure that it's all right to leave Eloise I'm off…and, in the meantime, don't be so quick to diagnose what ails me. I'm not in love with you,' she lied, 'so you can relax. A night on the town with people of my own age made me see that.'

She heard his quick intake of breath but his voice was

still calm as he said stiffly, 'Fair enough. Maybe now we'll be able to have the sort of relationship that a doctor should have with a trainee.'

'I'm sure that we will,' she promised sweetly, and before she disgraced herself by bursting into tears Nina turned the key in the lock and catapulted herself into the house.

The weeks after the midnight revelation passed uneventfully, except for one thing. Bettine Baker changed her name to Blackmore by marrying the father of the child she was carrying.

Nina heard one of the receptionists say that if it hadn't been for the hall he mightn't have been so willing, which made her think that they sounded a well-matched pair.

Bettine was still working in the practice. If the staff had thought that it might make for awkwardness, Rob and his ex-fiancée being thrown together on the job, his detached, cool politeness whenever they were in each other's company soon created an atmosphere devoid of rancour or embarrassment.

What his feelings really were with regard to Bettine no one knew, but it was noticed that he was absorbing himself in the practice even more than usual, was rarely seen out socially and that he looked tired and out of sorts.

His trainee didn't look much better, but as she wasn't of such interest to everyone as the no-longer-engaged senior partner, Nina's lack of zest went unnoticed by everyone but her stepmother.

Eloise had come back from her convalescence looking much better. She'd put on a little weight, her hair was growing again in a short boyish pelt and the sun and sea air had turned her pale skin to gold.

'You look lovely!' Nina had cried thankfully when she saw her.

As they'd hugged each other in the joy of reunion Eloise had said softly, 'And what about my girl? How have things been with you? Are you still eating your heart out for the handsome doctor who's promised to another?'

'Not now he isn't,' she'd said flatly. 'Rob found that his fiancée was pregnant by another man, and that was the end of that.'

Eloise's eyes had widened. 'So he's free!'

Nina's sigh had told her that it wasn't that simple. 'He's keeping his feelings under wraps, but he's made it quite clear that he's not in the market for a new model…such as yours truly.'

'So do we treat that as an ultimatum, or do we deduce that the delightful Robert protests too much?' her stepmother had asked.

'I'd put my money on the ultimatum theory,' Nina had told her, 'if his attitude towards me since it all came out into the open is anything to go by. He doesn't exactly treat me as if I've got the plague, but he's making sure I realize that he's out of bounds—for the likes of me, anyway.'

Eloise had known better than to try to comfort her with platitudes. She knew that the stepdaughter she loved was hurting…hurting badly. Nina had never been really in love before and she was finding the experience hard to handle, especially as she and Rob were teamed up at the practice, but it was something that she had to work through herself. No one else could do it for her.

As Bettine's pregnancy became more obvious by the day, Rob knew that his attitude was puzzling those around him. They must think him a cold fish to be accepting it so calmly, he thought with grim amusement.

Only he and the delectable young Nina knew that it had been over for him before Bettine's duplicity had come to light, and that his only regret was in not having finished with her sooner.

With regard to Nina, he was aware that her light had gone out and that he was in some degree to blame, but for the moment he wasn't prepared to do anything about it.

That night in the garden she'd questioned his integrity, and he'd had to explain the facts. It had been with reluctance as his private life was his own, but there had been no way he'd wanted her to think badly of him.

And so what had he done? Redeemed himself in one aspect of the messy business and then blighted their friendship by warning her off.

She'd retaliated by telling him that she didn't care for him and, although it had been what he'd wanted her to say, it had been a fitting finale to the worst few days of his life.

He was aware that Gavin was after her, and every time he saw the man hovering around Nina, Rob felt like telling the shallow charmer to lay off.

But having made it so clear that there wasn't going to be anything between Nina and himself, there wasn't a great deal he could do about it, except warn her.

His mouth twisted at the thought. It wasn't hard to imagine what sort of a reception that would get. 'Mind your own business' and 'Get out of my space' were two comments that came to mind.

If their personal relationship was a ragged sort of thing, not so their work in the practice. She was going to be a good doctor. Clever, confident and keen, he could rarely fault her.

He often thought wryly that the Bettine business had been good for the practice in that both he and Nina were so work-orientated these days that the other three partners had to run to keep up with them.

On a cool autumn morning a call came for them to visit the farmhouse that had been the setting for their first visit together on the day Nina had joined the practice.

As the car pulled out onto the hill road where the farm lay she eyed him warily. 'Wouldn't it have been better for one of the others to have taken this call?'

Rob shook his head. 'No. Tom Blackmore is my patient. The fact that his son impregnated my eager-beaver fiancée has no bearing on my commitment to his father.'

His voice was clipped and cold. She wanted to reach out and hold him. Tell him that she was aching for him all the time. But what he'd said that night in the darkened garden had left its mark. No way could she face being cut down to size again.

There were no freshly baked scones waiting for them today. Mary opened the door to them with a face pinched with anxiety.

'Thank you for coming, Dr Carslake,' she said, flustered at the sight of the man who had once been engaged to her new daughter-in-law. 'I hoped that it would be you that came to see Tom, but I suppose we couldn't blame you if you'd sent one of the others.'

'Don't worry about it, Mary,' he said quietly. 'Just tell me what the problem is. Is he worse?'

She nodded. 'Yes. He seems to be, but I called you out because he had a fall this morning. Tom was shuffling along like he does to the bathroom. Usually I'm there to help him, but he must have taken it into his head to go without me and he tripped over his dressing-gown cord which was trailing along the floor.'

Rob was already making for the stairs. 'He's in bed, I take it?' he said over his shoulder.

'Yes. I don't know how I managed to get him there, but I did. He's banged his head badly and is in a lot of pain with his wrist. It looks out of shape. I think it might be broken.'

As they went up the stairs, with Rob leading the way, Nina bringing up the rear and the farmer's wife sandwiched between, the young doctor was wondering where the new bridegroom-cum-father-to-be was.

For Rob's sake she hoped he didn't turn up while they were there. But would it matter if he did? The only comforting thing about the present state of affairs was that the man who was hurrying across to the big double bed with sudden urgency seemed to have no regrets about the disruption of his marriage plans.

'What is it?' Mary Blackmore cried as Rob bent over the sick man. 'What's wrong?'

By the time she reached Rob's side she could see for herself, and so could Nina. The farmer's eyes were gazing sightlessly up at the ceiling. His lips were blue and there was a film of froth on them.

As Rob felt the pulses in his neck and wrist he shook his head. 'He's gone, Mary,' he said gravely. 'How long is it since you left him?'

'Twenty minutes at the most,' she whispered tearfully.

'The fall did it, I imagine,' he told her as he examined the huge bruise on the dead man's temple.

His wife was weeping, great racking sobs, and as Nina held her close and tried to comfort her she surprised them both by saying, 'There's grief in me. We've been married forty-two years, but there's relief, too, that he's been taken. Tom has had no life for the past few years and it could have gone on and on.'

'Where are your sons?' Rob asked when they went downstairs again. 'Do they know about the fall?'

She shook her head. 'The two youngest are out in the pastures...and, as you know, Keith lives up at the hall now. Although, knowing him, he'll be engaged in the farm's business somewhere.'

Rob's face was devoid of expression as he said, 'Perhaps you'd like to phone the hall, Nina. If he's there ask him to come straight away.'

She nodded obediently. Of all the families to be involved with in such a manner, it had to be this one, she thought as she picked up the phone.

Miles answered, and when she asked for Keith she was in luck. 'Just a sec,' Bettine's brother said. 'I'll get him for you.'

There was silence after she'd imparted the sad news and then the farmer's oldest son barked, 'I'll be right over.' And that was that.

When she went back into the farmhouse kitchen it was to find that the younger Blackmores had come in for elevenses. The look on their mother's face and the presence of the two doctors were warning enough of what was to come.

After they'd absorbed the sad tidings one of them clomped slowly up the stairs to see his father, while the other took his mother in an awkward embrace.

'Has anybody told the "squire"?' he asked.

His mother nodded tearfully. 'Yes. The young doctor has phoned Keith. He's on his way.'

'I'm going to leave you a prescription for a sedative, Mary, just in case you need it,' Rob said as they prepared to leave. 'And there's one other thing. An autopsy is usually carried out when the cause of death isn't known. In your husband's case we do know what killed him. It was the Parkinson's disease, but his death was hastened by the fall.

'I don't think that the coroner's office will ask for an autopsy, but if you were willing to let one be performed so that the findings might be used in the treatment of the disease it could be arranged,' he said gently.

'Obviously you don't have to make a decision at this moment,' he added quietly. 'Think about it and let me know. We're going to leave you with your family now, but if there's anything at all that we at the practice can do, be sure to let me know.'

As they drove to their next call, with the morning now well spent, Nina said hesitantly, 'I imagine you're feeling that you could have done without that?'

He smiled. 'It's all part of a day's work, Nina. It might have been better for the Blackmores if Bettine had answered the call, either in the guise of daughter-in-law or GP, but as it was they got me.'

'Us.'

'Yes, my apologies…us.'

'And none of it bothered you?'

'The old man's death bothered me. It's always sad to lose a patient but, as his wife said, it's a relief, too. He was in a very bad state. As for the rest of it, presuming that you're referring to the Bettine business, I don't give a damn. I thought I'd made that clear to you on a previous occasion.'

'You made a lot of things clear to me on a previous occasion,' Nina said, grasping at the opportunity to push to one side the polite reserve she'd been fretting behind for weeks.

'Yes. I believe I did.'

'Oh! So you haven't forgotten?'

'Of course I haven't forgotten! It isn't exactly easy, working with you and keeping my distance at the same time.'

'So why do you?'

There was a lay-by ahead and he pulled into it, saying as he did so, 'I can't carry on this sort of a discussion while I'm driving.'

'Why not?' she snapped with the aggression still in her.

Incredibly, Rob was smiling. 'Supposing I want my hands free.'

'Huh! That'll be the day but, then, I'm forgetting. *I'm* not the one with the touch-me-not complex, am I? I'm not allowed to make advances to you, but if the mood takes you…!'

'How do you know that the mood doesn't take me a hundred times a day?' he said, his good humour changing to gravity. 'That I'm continually reminding myself that I've already been involved in one nine-day wonder and that I don't want to drag you into another.'

'Why don't you let me be the judge of whether I'm prepared for that to happen? And if it was merely a nine-day wonder, what's the problem?'

'The problem is that you're young, very beautiful and somewhat scatty. A natural-born risk-taker… And I'm not. Not when it comes to those under my jurisdiction.'

'So how would it be if I changed my job? They're advertising for a waitress at the Gun and Target.'

'And waste all that talent? Come here, Nina.'

He reached across and, putting his hand under her chin, turned her face to his. 'I'm going to regret this, I know. It would be so much easier if you played hard to get.'

When his lips took hers all the misery of the last few weeks was wiped out. His kisses were as strong and demanding as the man himself. Yet the hands that were holding her had the safest touch she'd ever known.

He released her at last, and as his hands fell away and his mouth left hers Rob groaned, 'We're miles behind with the calls, Nina. What am I thinking of? I told you I'd regret it!'

'Yes, you did, didn't you?' she said lifelessly. 'You'd better start the car.'

'I didn't mean it like that,' he protested, his eyes on her set face.

'No? Then how did you mean it?' And as he opened his mouth to speak she held up her hand. 'Shush! You've said enough.'

When they got back to the practice Bettine had just returned from her rounds. Judging from her expression, the Blackmores hadn't been in touch.

'Have you got a minute?' Rob said as Nina went into the kitchen to put the kettle on.

'Yes, of course,' Bettine said gushingly.

'I have some bad news,' he told her, taking her to one side.

'Nothing's happened to Miles...or Keith, has it?' she asked quickly.

'No. It's your father-in-law. He had a bad fall this morning and Mary called us out, but he had died before we got there.'

'Oh, no!' she cried and flung herself, weeping, into his arms.

As Nina came out of the kitchen with a steaming brew

Rob was patting Bettine's shoulder gently and murmuring words of comfort.

Nina was ashamed to admit it, but she was angry. If Bettine was flopping about in anybody's arms it should have been her husband's, not putting on a big show of emotion for Rob's benefit.

She'd only been part of the Blackmore family for a matter of weeks, certainly not long enough to be prostrated with grief, and she'd forfeited any right to seek solace in the embrace of the man that she herself loved to distraction.

Why, for goodness' sake, wasn't he gently but firmly telling her to go to her in-laws, instead of drooping all over him and wetting the front of his shirt?

Rob had seen her expression and his eyes were saying, All right, calm down. I'm merely offering the same comfort I would to anyone suffering a bereavement.

But it wasn't anyone, was it? It was Bettine, and with a toss of her russet crop Nina went into her room and closed the door.

It had barely had time to settle on its hinges before it was opening again to admit Gavin. He nodded in the direction from which he'd come. 'What's all that about?' he asked. 'Not young Miles, is it?'

'No. Her father-in-law has died. We were called out to him this morning, but when we got there it was too late.'

'And so either Bettine was very fond of him or she's missing Roberto's attentions more than somewhat,' he remarked. 'What to you think?'

'I think your second theory applies.'

'And you're not happy?'

'Er...no.'

'You still fancy him, don't you? That's why I can't

get a look-in. You know that you're wasting your time, don't you? After the Bettine affair I'm surprised he didn't go into a monastery. Rob Carslake is somewhat cheesed off with your sex.'

'All right!' Nina snapped, with the memory still rankling of the weeping Bettine in Rob's arms. 'You don't have to lay it on with a trowel.'

CHAPTER SEVEN

THE next morning, as Nina and one of the practice nurses were waiting for patients to turn up for cervical smear tests, Barbara asked from behind the reception counter, 'Does anyone know where Dr Carslake is? He has an appointment in fifteen minutes with a rep from one of the big pharmaceutical companies.'

Gavin and Vikram were both around. Bettine had rung in to say she would be in later, and Rob had finished his morning surgery half an hour ago, but now he wasn't to be seen.

'I believe he went up to the flat,' Vikram said.

'I've rung through on the internal phone and there was no answer,' the receptionist said, 'but the phones are playing up this morning. I'll have to get on to the phone company.'

'I'll pop up and give him the message if you like,' Nina offered, and before anyone else could pip her to the post she headed for the stairs, thinking as she did so that this was going to be a first, seeing the inside of the flat, providing, of course, that she wasn't kept standing on the mat.

Rob was familiar enough with her home, but in all the weeks she'd been working at the practice she'd never set foot in his, and, needless to say, she was curious.

He'd nodded briefly in her direction before surgery and there'd been a note on her desk to say that he felt she was now competent enough to do her own visits.

After reading it, she'd experienced a longing to be

back on their more friendly footing, and if running errands for Reception would do the trick, then errand girl she would be.

'Yes, what is it?' Rob asked when he opened the door to her, with an excited Zacky barking in the background.

'Can I come in?' she asked.

He stepped back. 'Yes, of course, though I can't think what you might want of me.'

She was sorely tempted to tell him what she wanted of him, but it wasn't the right moment, and with a tight laugh she said, 'You obviously haven't got "Welcome" written on your mat.'

'Can we get to the point, please, Nina?'

'Yes. Reception asked me to remind you about an appointment with a pharmaceutical rep.'

'I see. Phones not working?'

'No, as a matter of fact, they're not. Barbara is getting on to the phone company.'

'That's all we need. A doctor's surgery without telephone communication! Thanks for the message.'

Nina was only half listening. She was looking around her, taking in the spartan accommodation of the flat above the surgery.

He saw her expression and almost smiled. 'What is it? Were you expecting something more luxurious? If you were, you're doomed to disappointment as the rest of it is no better than this, I'm afraid.'

The furniture was good, solid stuff, but old. The polished wooden floors were attractive in their own way, but they would have looked drab without the scattering of brightly coloured rugs.

The paintings were the only things of class, vivid watercolours of local scenes and people that were so vibrantly alive she caught her breath.

'Whatever the decor of the flat lacks, the paintings make up for it,' she said. 'Who's the artist?'

'*Moi*,' he said with an exaggerated continental-type bow.

'You!' she breathed. 'You've painted all these, Rob? What a talent!'

He laughed. 'I'm glad you approve of something I've done.'

'I approve of everything about you,' she said softly, 'except—'

'When I start fussing over my ex-fiancée? Your expression was something to be seen. What did you expect me to do? Push her away? Make light of a death in her husband's family? The least I could do was offer some comfort.'

'I knew you were going to bring that up,' she said stiffly, 'and I'm sorry that I made my feelings so obvious.'

'You certainly did,' he agreed. 'How do you think *I* feel when I see Gavin hovering around you? But I don't make a public announcement of my disapproval.'

It was her turn to break into what he was saying. 'You're about to warn me that he's bad news? That the golden-haired Gavin isn't to be trusted?'

'Something like that.'

'I'm aware of the fact.'

'And yet you're still prepared to let him hang around you?'

'Maybe. At least he does want my company.'

'And you think I don't?'

'That's how it looks.'

'Yes, well, looks aren't everything. You're old enough to know that.'

He then took the wind out of her sails by saying suddenly, 'Are you going to the fair?'

'Fair?'

'Yes, the September fair. It arrives in one of the fields at the back of the village on Friday night and stays until Monday.'

Nina's eyes sparkled. 'I'll have to ask Gavin to take me,' she teased.

'No need for that,' Rob said calmly. 'I'll take you myself...on Saturday night...if you're free. It's one way of making sure that you don't get carried off by gypsies.'

'You mean like the lady in the story of the raggle-taggle gypsies? Except that she went of her own free will.'

'No. I mean as in the story of Nina Lombard who isn't cut out for caravan life.'

'Oh, I don't know. If the gypsy was handsome enough I suppose I could get used to it,' she said with the sparkle still in evidence, but now it was there because they were friends again...and unbelievably Rob was going to take her to the fair!

He reached out and touched her face gently and she became still. 'Forget the people of the road, Nina,' he said softly. 'There are enough of us here who would like you to share our caravans, but circumstances get in the way sometimes.'

'There's no reason why they should,' she told him, looking him straight in the eye.

As he opened his mouth to answer, Barbara's voice intruded. 'The ladies for the smear tests are all here, Dr Lombard,' she called up the stairs, and with a sigh Nina went to carry out yet another part of a GP's busy schedule.

*   *   *

For the rest of the week Nina was totally happy. Saturday was like a beacon shining on her horizon. This would be their first proper date, she kept telling herself.

Eloise was watching her. Nina had told her that she was going to the fair with Rob, so she knew the reason for her young stepdaughter's high spirits and prayed they weren't going to be the forerunner of a fall.

Nina's father hadn't been let into the secret. His reactions were often difficult to cope with. The last thing Nina wanted was for him to ask Rob what his intentions were, and he would if the mood took him.

Yet if he did do that, embarrassing though it might be, her dad could be doing her a favour, as she would like to know what his intentions were, too. He'd made them quite clear on a few occasions and then out of the blue he'd offered to take her to the fair.

'Shall I call for you tomorrow night?' Rob asked as they saw off the last patient on the Friday.

Did he guess that she didn't want her father poking his nose in? she wondered. Or was he just as anxious as she that the weakening of his resolve shouldn't be made public, if 'weakening' was a word one would use in connection with the man who was quick enough to diagnose what *she* was suffering from, but not as quick to sound out his own heart.

'No. As the surgery is nearer to where they're holding the fair, I'll call for you,' she volunteered. 'What time do you suggest?'

'Half six to sevenish? It will be dark by then.'

As she drove home, the thought of strolling around the brightly lit fairground in the dark autumn night with Rob was all she could think of.

It was only later, as she lay dreamily watching a yellow moon through her bedroom window, that it occurred to her that his comment that it would be dark by the time they got there might have something to do with the fact that he still wasn't happy about being seen with her outside the practice.

She pushed the thought away. If that was the case, why had he made the arrangement? If Rob was dubious about them being seen together, she certainly wasn't. What was more, she would sort out the brightest clothes in her wardrobe for tomorrow night so that she *would* be seen.

When Nina arrived at the surgery the following evening, Rob had just got back from walking Zacky and he said with a rueful smile, 'This young fellow didn't like all the racket that's going on around the fair. He was almost as jumpy as on Bonfire Night.'

As Nina bent to stroke the quivering animal he said, 'You look positively dazzling!'

'Do I?' she asked mock-innocently. 'Is that a compliment or just a mere statement of fact?'

'A bit of both,' he replied calmly. 'They'll be able to turn off the lights when you get to the fair.'

'Very funny.'

Tight emerald green trousers and a tangerine-coloured tunic, offset with a multicoloured scarf knotted stylishly at the neck, were providing the effect she wanted, and with gold sandals on her feet and a matching bag there was no way she would go unnoticed among the crowd at the fair.

In contrast, whether by accident or design, Rob was dressed in a dark brown shirt and jeans, and Nina thought whimsically, The moth and the butterfly went to the fair on a beautiful autumn night...

He was watching her face. 'What's the joke?'

'Nothing.'

'Hmm,' he murmured dubiously. 'I don't believe that! But the plan isn't to stand chatting all night, so let's be off.'

As was the way with fairs, the spectacle that had been erected on the field on the outskirts of the village had attracted far more people than the residents of Stepping Dearsley. Young and old alike had been drawn to the cluster of rides and sideshows as if by a magnet.

Rob had been right about the noise—it was deafening. Yet it was exciting, too, in its own raucous way.

If he hadn't wanted them to be on view, he'd brought her to the wrong place, Nina thought as they strolled among the jostling crowd. They were being stopped by people who knew Rob all the time, and it wasn't surprising.

Who was better known in the village than Rob Carslake? The people in the post office maybe, or the local bobby, but after that came the practice—and Rob Carslake *was* the practice. She'd had no need to dress up like a beacon. His popularity and the very nature of his function among them meant that he wouldn't go unobserved.

He won a coconut and presented it to her with a boyish grin, and as they moved around, with Nina holding it in one hand and a mass of pink candyfloss in the other, she found him watching her with smiling intentness.

Looking up at the big Ferris wheel towering against the skyline, he said, 'Shall we?'

'Mmmm,' she replied, 'and then I'd like to go on the Dodgems, the Caterpillar and—'

He'd taken her arm and was propelling her towards the ticket box. 'One thing at a time, my sweet.'

Her eyes widened at the endearment, if that was what it had been. It didn't describe her, though, did it? She wasn't 'sweet'. These days she was more often sour, and whose fault was it if she was more of an acid drop than a bon-bon?

It was exhilarating, just the two of them in the swaying seat as it rose higher and higher above the fairground. She could have stayed in it for ever, and when it got to the highest point it looked as if that was going to be the case as the seats all came to a standstill.

As the minutes ticked by and there was no further movement Rob said whimsically, 'It would seem that we have a technical fault. What does it feel like to be marooned up in the sky?'

'Wonderful,' she said softly. Her green eyes pleading that he might feel the same.

'If I'd wanted to take you somewhere away from the eyes and ears of the world, I couldn't have chosen a better place, could I?' he teased.

Nina looked over the edge of the seat. 'I'd say we were pretty much on view.'

'Maybe, but not so much as who we are...and what we're doing.

'Why, what are we doing?' she asked, wide-eyed.

Rob laughed and it had a carefree, boyish sound to it. 'Nothing yet. But given time...and space...'

He was leaning forward and taking her hands in his. Then, carefully pulling her towards him, he said, 'I've never kissed a beautiful woman at this altitude before, and in a rocking wooden seat...'

It's working! Nina thought triumphantly. Rob was accepting that there was this thing between them that couldn't be ignored. He felt it just as much as she did, and she didn't care where they were, up in the sky or at

the bottom of the local pit, the fact that they were together and he wanted her was all that mattered.

But something else was working, too. The great wheel
was turning again, and as they began the downward de-
scent Rob released her hands and sat back in his seat.

'So it's been sorted out,' he said unsmilingly. 'We're
on our way back to ground level...and sanity.'

'It's clear to see that you're hugely relieved to have
been spared from making a fool of yourself,' Nina
snapped as hurt and disappointment gave way to anger.
'If your mind was as quick to sort out what's going on
in there as the fairground staff were in getting the wheel
in motion again, I might feel less used and confused!'

They were now at ground level, and when he reached
out to help her out of the seat she pushed his hand away
and strode past him.

'Hey! What's all this, then?' he asked as he caught
up with her.

'As if you need ask,' she cried. 'Why is that every
time you succumb to the attraction between us, you act
as if you've escaped a fate worse than death when the
moment is interrupted?'

'You underestimate my feelings,' Rob said with a
chill in his voice to match her own. 'I don't feel as if
I've escaped an unpleasant fate at all. It's more like having had to pass by the entrance to heaven.'

'Then why—?'

'You know why. I've already told you.'

'The trouble with you, Rob,' she flared, 'is that you're
too blinkered to see what's staring you in the face.
You're letting the past threaten the future! I'm going
home...and don't offer to come with me because I don't
want you to.'

When she got to the end of the road Nina looked back.

The huge wheel, now revolving smoothly, was silhouetted against the night sky.

What would have happened if the fairground staff had taken longer to repair it? Would she and Rob have reached a stage where all the rules he'd set himself had been swept away? Or would it have been as before—just a case of her being ready and available?

When she got in Nina found Eloise lying on the couch in the sitting room. The tan she'd acquired from her two weeks by the sea had faded, and in that moment she looked frail and weary.

'What is it, darling?' Nina asked anxiously, her own problems immediately put to one side.

'Nothing,' Eloise replied in answer to Nina's concern. 'I couldn't sleep, so I went for a stroll around the garden and then came in here.'

'Can I get you anything?'

Eloise shook her head. 'No. But what you *can* do is tell me what sort of an evening you've had.'

Nina pulled a face. 'Good up to a point, then disappointing.'

When she explained about the mechanical fault on the wheel her stepmother said laughingly, 'Are you sure you didn't slip them something to have it break down when it did?'

'Surprisingly, I never thought of it,' she confessed wryly, 'or I might have done. Not that it would have made any difference. Every time Rob and I are together he gets all moral. As if he's the epitome of wisdom and I'm a complete scatterbrain.'

'How old is Dr Carslake?'

'Thirty-five.'

'So there is a small gap.'

'Hmm. For what it matters.'

'I'm sorry that he's in no hurry to return your feelings,' Eloise said gently, 'but give him time, Nina. The man has just had an unpleasant experience with a rather callous woman.'

'Who I think now wishes she hadn't been so eager to jump into bed with someone else. Bettine still wants him. I can feel it in my bones,' Nina said wretchedly.

'What! And she's carrying this other fellow's child! She hasn't a chance,' Eloise consoled. 'Rob Carslake is nobody's pushover.'

'Tell me about it,' Nina groaned. 'But enough of my affairs. What about you? Are you coming to bed?'

Eloise shook her head. 'No. I'm going to spend the night down here on the sofa. It's cooler. You could get me a glass of squash if you will, in case I'm thirsty during the night. And, Nina…you know that I'm seeing the consultant again on Friday?'

'Yes, of course.'

'And that the news could be good…or very bad?'

'Yes. I know that, too. The thought is always at the forefront of my mind.'

'Mine, too,' Eloise said solemnly, 'and I want you to promise me something in these few quiet moments together.'

'What is it?' Nina asked with the familiar feeling of dread that never left her.

'If anything happens to me, as it does to lots of folk when the chemotherapy is stopped or hasn't worked, I want you to promise not to grieve. I can only depart this world peacefully if I know that you accept my going without devastation.'

Nina's face had blanched. She knelt down beside the wasted figure of her stepmother and took her hand. 'How

can I not grieve, my darling Eloise? You mean everything to me.'

The sick woman stroked her hair with a gentle hand.
'Yes. I know I do and that's why I'm asking this of you.
If and when the time comes, be glad for me, Nina. So
that I can go in peace.'

'Don't talk like this,' her stepdaughter begged. 'I can't
bear it.'

'I have to, Nina. It's the sensible thing to do.'

'What about Dad?' Nina asked desperately. 'What's
he going to be like if ever anything happens to you?'

'Abrasive, demanding, bewildered, but domesticity
never did suit him. He was happier in a man's world
and he'll cope. His army training will be of more use to
him then than it's ever been.

'You're the one I'm worried about. I wish to goodness
your delightful doctor would get his act together. But I
haven't gone yet, have I? Who knows?'

As Nina went slowly up the stairs she was thinking
that the way things were going between Rob and herself
he was going to end up a crusty old bachelor and she
would be the hanger-on, waiting for the occasional
crumb that he might throw. But what did all that matter
compared to what might happen to Eloise?

'I want to talk to you,' she told him first thing Monday
morning.

Rob was going through the mail and his head came
up sharply at the sound of her voice.

'Oh! So we *are* on speaking terms, then?'

She couldn't be bothered to answer him. For the last
two nights she hadn't slept a wink for thinking about
Eloise, and if there was one person who might be able
to calm her tortuous thoughts it was he.

He was observing the shadows beneath her eyes and the weary droop of her mouth, and when he spoke again there was no flippancy in his voice.

'What's wrong, Nina? You look dreadful.'

'Eloise is talking about dying. She goes to see the consultant on Friday and doesn't seem very hopeful that there will be good news.'

'Why is that, do you think?' he said slowly. 'They said the last time that the cancer was stable.'

'Yes. I know they did, and I don't know whether it's because the chemo has made her feel so weak and ill that she's thinking on those lines, or if she has a premonition.'

He was frowning. 'That isn't an unusual situation with cancer patients. The weeks spent on treatment must seem like a frightening limbo. The thought of it being fatal will always be there no matter how positive their thinking.'

'Yes, you're right, of course. Thanks, Rob. Just talking to you has helped,' she said tearfully.

He held out his arms and she went into them like a ship into harbour. 'If I could ease the burden for you all I would,' he murmured with his lips against her hair, 'but they're doing all they can at the oncology unit... The rest is in the lap of the gods.'

They were as physically close as they'd ever been in this quiet moment before surgery, but it was a time for comfort rather than passion and, releasing her, Rob said gently, 'Go and get a cup of tea before the day starts or you'll be the next one I'm called out to.'

As the daily procession of the sick and suffering came and went with its mixture of the serious and simple in health care, Nina was grateful for the concentration required.

Over the weekend there had been nothing to occupy her mind but Eloise's problems, but now, back in the surgery, and with Rob only a few feet away, her resilience was returning.

Their relationship might not be going anywhere, but he'd been tender and caring earlier when he'd seen her distress, and it had meant a lot.

The old man who'd been coughing up blood was one of her first patients of the day. The results of the tests that she'd asked for had come through, and Reception had phoned to ask him to come in without delay.

'So what have I got, Doctor?' he asked, with the resignation of the old who knew they weren't going to live for ever. 'Was I right about the gallopin' consumption?'

Nina nodded. 'Yes. You've got tuberculosis, if that's what you mean.'

'So they'll be sticking me in a hut on some mountainside then, while me lungs recover?'

She smiled. She liked this down-to-earth, elderly man, but he'd been a bit sparse with information on his first visit.

'No. We've moved on a bit since those days,' she told him. 'I'll be prescribing a strong course of antibiotics.'

'It's what they did to me before,' he persisted.

'What?'

'Stuck me in a cabin on a mountain.'

'Why didn't you tell me that you'd had it before?'

'I did.'

'I don't think so.'

'I *said* was it gallopin' consumption.'

'And I was supposed to deduce from that comment that you'd had TB before? I'm not a mind-reader, you know, and your notes don't go that far back.'

'It was a long time ago. I caught it when I was in the army, just after the war.'

'I see. Well, the X-rays that you had at the hospital showed up the scars on your lungs from before and, as can happen, even after many years, the illness has flared up again.'

'So do I need to start putting me affairs in order?' he asked with a twinkle in his eyes.

'Not just yet. But do make sure that you take the medication.'

He was followed by another senior citizen, this time accompanied by her daughter. Dorothy Desmond was an amazing woman. Ninety-nine years of age, and mentally as sharp as a needle, the old lady was beginning to fail physically now.

On a recent stay in a care home while her daughter had a holiday, she had slipped and fallen and was now complaining of severe pain at the top of her leg and around the hip area.

'I wouldn't mind, but it's my good leg that I've hurt,' she said. 'I reached out for the buggy that I lean on when I'm walking and it tipped over. What do you think of that?'

'I think that it's most unfortunate,' Nina told her. 'I'm going to examine you and then I'm going to ask Dr Carslake to come in and have a look at you as I'm still training and may not be qualified enough to make a judgement on just how badly you've hurt yourself.'

As Dorothy's daughter helped her off with her tights Nina saw that both Dorothy's legs were bandaged. Pointing to them, she asked, 'Are those injuries from the fall?'

The old lady shook her head. 'No. It's my skin. It's

that old it's like tissue paper. The slightest knock and it breaks.'

It was clear that Dorothy was in a lot of pain, but the fact that she could walk seemed to cancel out any fractures and Nina went to find Rob.

'I think that we need to send you for X-rays, Mrs Desmond,' he told her. 'You appear to be mobile enough, but I'm not happy with the amount of pain that you're experiencing.' He turned to her daughter. 'Do you have transport?'

'Yes, I do, but my mother, being in the state she is, can't twist round to get into the car.'

He nodded. 'Yes. I can see that could be a problem.' To Nina he added, 'Will you ask Reception to phone for an ambulance, Dr Lombard?'

Today was antenatal day again, and Bettine, who was in charge, was at her most officious. By the time they were ready to start seeing the patients she'd snapped at the community midwife who was assisting them and weighed herself twice, stepping off the scales with a face like stone.

That had brought forth smiles from those assisting her and a whispered comment from the affronted midwife that those who didn't want a bump at the front shouldn't play with fire.

Bettine had also complained that there weren't enough disposable sheets for the pregnant women to lie on, which might have been the case had they been the clinic of the town's main maternity unit but as there were only six mothers-to-be present Nina was hard put not to challenge Bettine's counting capabilities.

She hadn't mellowed much by the time the clinic was

over and if Nina had liked her better she might have sympathised with her situation.

There was young Miles for whom she was responsible up to a point, her grieving mother-in-law in the background and a husband who couldn't possibly match up to Robert Carslake...plus a child on the way that had been conceived in surreptitious circumstances.

As Rob had held Nina in his arms and stroked her hair before surgery he'd been acutely aware of the fine-boned slenderness of her and the tangy smell of her perfume. But more than those things he'd been conscious of the need in her.

There had been the wetness of tears on her cheeks. Every line of her beautiful, coltish body had been crying out for comfort. Flippant she sometimes was, overconfident, even stroppy on occasion, but there was a great capacity for love inside Nina Lombard. It was there in the way she felt about Eloise. It would be there for the man she married one day. But that was a subject that he chose not to dwell on at the present time.

The problem was that having made that decision he was finding it very difficult to keep to it. Nina was a tantalising young witch for one thing, and for another her stepmother hadn't actually spelled it out but she'd dropped some heavy hints that she would like to see her married before anything happened.

That he'd been cast in the role of bridegroom had been plain to see and he would have been furious if the prompting had come from anyone else, but Eloise Lombard was a different matter.

Feeling restless and on edge, he went up to the flat when morning surgery was over and as he went in his glance went to where a half-finished oil painting lay on his easel.

The green eyes looking out at him from there were clear and sparkling. The dark russet mop framed a laughing face, a far cry from the tearful girl who'd made him feel weak with tenderness when he'd held her in his arms earlier.

He sighed. Instead of being his usual playful self, Zacky was snapping around his ankles. He'd had to take the Border terrier to the vet over the weekend to have an infected foot treated, so there were no rainbows on his horizon either.

CHAPTER EIGHT

IT WAS November. The nights were drawing in, the mornings decidedly chilly, and where usually the changing seasons rarely bothered him Rob knew that he wasn't looking forward to this winter.

He'd handled the attraction between Nina and himself all wrong, and now he felt that anything else he might say in mitigation would only make matters worse. Which meant that dark days, coupled with bleak thoughts, were making him feel less than cheerful.

Whenever he heard anyone mention Christmas his gloom increased. Would the Lombards have Eloise with them for Christmas? he wondered. He hoped so. There'd been nothing worse to report on her last check-up, and he prayed that in spite of the fact that she was feeling weak and ill and was having gloomy premonitions, the forthcoming consultation would have no less progress to report than the last.

The staff were getting ready to put up the Christmas decorations in the surgery and there was much talk of pre-festive shopping, but he noticed that although Nina listened, she didn't join in.

He hated to see her sparkle missing, but he would have thought less of her if it hadn't been. There were times when he felt that she was maturing before his eyes, yet it was sad that the way of it should be so painful for her.

Gavin had finally given up on her because she was proving such poor company. The blond charmer preferred the lighter side of life, and in his eyes Nina Lombard was about as exciting as a church jumble sale these days.

Rob was keeping his distance, too, but for very different reasons. He'd made sure that Nina knew he was there if she needed him, both as doctor and friend. He felt that any other approach would neither be wanted nor in good taste.

If she sought the comfort of his arms again they would be waiting for her. But there was no way he was going to use her present vulnerability for his own ends.

Fortunately, practice matters were there to keep him from brooding, and on the Tuesday morning of that week he had a phone call asking him to make a home visit to Dorothy Desmond, the ninety-nine-year-old he'd sent to hospital for X-rays after a fall.

Her daughter opened the door to him, her face creased with anxiety. 'My mother is in an awful lot of pain, Doctor,' she told him as he stepped into the hallway.

'What did they say at the hospital?' he enquired.

She smiled tiredly. 'She's broken her pelvis in three places. Can you believe it? I leave her for a couple of weeks and we end up with this.'

'Is that the doctor?' the old lady called from the other room.

'Yes, it is, Mrs Desmond,' Rob replied as he proceeded into her small sitting room.

'Has Pauline told you what I've done?' she asked. He nodded. 'They've told me I've just got to let the fractures heal naturally. That it's like broken ribs. There's nothing they can do. But in the meantime I'm in a lot of pain and wondered if you could give me something for it.'

'Of course, and I must say that you're a very brave lady, coping with something like this at your age.'

Bright eyes were twinkling up at him from a sunken face. 'I'm ready to go, you know, Doctor. I keep telling the nurse when she comes to change the bandages on my legs that I'm in favour of euthanasia, but she doesn't take any notice.'

When he was leaving, after making out a prescription for painkillers, Pauline Desmond said, 'She doesn't mean it, you know...about the euthanasia. Mum has got all her cards and presents for Christmas and is looking forward to going to a family wedding. It's just her little joke.'

As Rob made his way back to the practice he wasn't to know that Nina was thinking along the same lines as him. The job was saving her sanity, she thought frequently.

Apart from its many other duties, dealing with her share of the patients in the morning and afternoon surgeries was a constant reminder that Eloise wasn't the only one with serious medical problems.

Brian Benyon, the local butcher, was a case in point. He'd been diagnosed with multiple sclerosis in his early twenties. Blurred vision and tingling of the hands and feet had prodded him towards his GP, and tests had shown that MS was present.

The original symptoms had cleared up with drugs, and for a few years he'd been almost free of discomfort. There'd been the odd hiccup but nothing to be alarmed about until now, and Reception had passed him on to her on a cold, grey morning.

His wife was with him, and Nina could almost feel the tension in them as they came into her consulting room. 'I might have known I was doing too well,' the butcher mumbled as he lowered himself into one of the chairs opposite her desk. 'What's going to happen to the business? That's what I want to know!'

With a feeling that she was missing something, Nina said, 'Let's start at the beginning shall we, Mr Benyon? What's the problem?'

He stared at her. 'Haven't you read my notes, then?'

'Yes. I have. I see that you have MS. Is that what you've come about?'

'What else?'

She was tempted to say that it could have been an ingrowing toenail, but restrained herself. The man was obviously in a state, and MS was no joke in anyone's book.

'It's his arms, Doctor,' his wife said. 'The use keeps going out of them...and he's got a business to run. He can hardly hold a knife, and as for a cleaver...no chance!'

This was the old story of multiple sclerosis, Nina thought. In most cases there were long periods when the disease was dormant. Then suddenly it would flare up in a mild or more virulent form, as if to remind the sufferer that it was still a force to be reckoned with.

From this man's notes it was obvious that he'd had a clear run for many years, and now it looked as if it was reminder time.

As she examined him Nina saw that there was weakness, especially in the upper arms. She'd also noticed that he'd been limping when he'd come in.

'What about your leg? Is that bothering you, too?' she questioned.

'Aye, it is,' he grunted, 'but I don't cut the meat up with me legs.'

She ignored that remark and commented, 'I see from

your notes that you have twice-yearly appointments with the hospital and that the last one was three months ago. Were you having this trouble then?'

He shook his head. 'Naw. It only started last week.'

'I see. Well, I'm afraid I'm going to have to refer you back to them, Mr Benyon. It looks as if the MS has flared up again. They'll probably prescribe corticosteroid drugs, but first they'll check the progression of the disease with magnetic resonance imaging.'

'They've done that before,' Brian's wife said. He looked at her blankly. 'When they put you in that tube. Don't you remember?'

'Oh, aye. I didn't like it either. I'm too claustrophobic for that sort of thing.'

'I'll ask them to give you an early appointment,' Nina told him. 'And, in the meantime, try not to worry. The symptoms of MS often die down just as quickly as they've flared up.'

'If you say so, Doctor,' he agreed doubtfully, and off they went, back to the sides of beef and sausages, with the future a grey area and the past something that he'd taken for granted and was only now beginning to be grateful for.

When Nina got home that night she was amazed to find that Eloise and her father had been shopping. In the other woman's weakened state it was incredible that she'd found the strength, but she had, and the dining table was strewn with parcels.

'I've been doing my Christmas shopping,' she said with a tired smile as Nina goggled at the array.

There was a choking feeling in her throat. Eloise was full of doubts about the future, but she'd still made the effort. If her stepmother could do it, then *she* should throw off her melancholy and do the same.

'It's late-night shopping in town tomorrow night,' she said to Rob the following morning. 'I'm going to get some Christmas shopping done before Eloise has her ordeal on Friday.'

Why she was telling him she really didn't know, unless she'd been hoping that he might suggest going with her, but there was no immediate offer.

'Good for you,' he said, giving her a quick sideways glance.

'Eloise has done hers,' she explained, 'which makes me feel that I must do mine.'

He smiled. 'That lady is something else.'

'Isn't she just? Have you done *your* shopping?' she asked, apparently in all innocence.

'Sort of. I buy gifts for the staff, usually chocolates or wine that come straight from the wholesalers, and with regard to personal gifts I've only one to concern myself with and it's all organised.'

She eyed him curiously, 'Haven't you got any family, Rob?'

He shook his head. 'No. My father died during a dreadful flu epidemic when I was quite small and I lost my mother last year. Before you ask, it was cancer.'

'Oh, Rob!' she breathed as tenderness welled up inside her. 'I didn't know.'

He smiled. 'Well, of course you didn't. There was no reason you should.'

'Yes, but you've been there for me all the time I've been agonising over Eloise. I hope there was someone there for you. Bettine maybe?'

He shook his head. 'No. At that time she'd only just joined the practice. I coped, Nina. I *am* a GP, you know.'

'So am I, but it doesn't make it any easier.'

'That's true, it doesn't. But what I went through has helped me to understand how you're feeling.'

'I can't bear to think of you being all alone in the world,' she said softly. 'Yet you're so self-sufficient. You never seem as if you need anyone else in your life.'

'Don't you believe it. I'm as weak as the next man,' he said laughingly.

'That statement is a complete fabrication. You have a will of iron.'

He took a step towards her. 'Shall I prove you wrong? Or do you think it's a little too public here for that kind of demonstration?'

Nina could have told him that she didn't care if half the village were watching as long as he wanted her, but that kind of approach belonged to her old image. The new one had more restraint. So she said nothing.

Rob didn't pursue the matter and there was still laughter in him as he said, 'I haven't any urgent shopping to do, but I suppose I could go with you. I don't like to think of you being alone with all that you have on your mind. We could take my car and travel in together.'

A few weeks ago she would have been saying yes before he'd got the words out, but she felt as if she'd aged a hundred years since the night they'd been marooned on the big wheel.

Therefore, it was with apparently casual acceptance that she took him up on his suggestion. It was only when she got home that she allowed herself to dwell on the pleasure ahead. At the same time berating herself for not allowing that moment in the surgery to develop as it might have done.

*   *   *

'I'm thinking of going late-night shopping with Rob to-night, straight from the practice,' she told Eloise next morning. 'Will you be all right?'

'Yes, of course I will,' her stepmother said firmly when she saw Nina's indecision. 'Go and do your shopping...and don't rush back. If you've got the chance to spend some time with Rob Carslake...don't pass it by.'

'So, are we all set to buy up the town?' Rob asked as they pulled off the practice forecourt that evening. Dark eyes in the face that was never out of her mind were looking her over approvingly, 'You look stunning, Dr Lombard.'

Nina smiled. In a short black jacket with a fur collar, tight leather pants and a white poloneck sweater that clung to her slender throat and the globes of her breasts, she was making a fashion statement, and it was gratifying that it hadn't gone unnoticed.

'You don't look so bad yourself,' she said in return, but when had his appearance not made her heart beat faster? Whether in the business suits that he wore at the practice, or in the jeans and casual shirt he'd worn on the night of the fair, the effect was always impressive.

Rob's sheepskin coat sat comfortably across his broad shoulders and the shirt and tie beneath it were a smart match for tailored worsted trousers. Today the moth and the butterfly were absent. It was the country squire and the city girl venturing forth.

For Eloise Nina bought the prettiest nightgown and matching bed jacket she could find, and for her father a set of bowls as he'd recently taken a fancy to the game.

There was one other gift she wanted to buy, but as its recipient was strolling along beside her in the town's biggest shopping mall it wasn't going to be easy unless he had somewhere else to go. He'd said the previous day that his Christmas shopping was organised, so the odds were that he was going to be with her all the time.

However, almost as if he'd read her thoughts Rob said suddenly, 'I have some business to attend to that will take me about half an hour. Where shall we meet?'

'In the coffee-shop across the way,' she suggested, and off he went, standing out in the jostling throng like the bright beacon in her life that he was.

Once he'd gone came the next problem. What to get him? Something for his spartan flat would be a good idea. It wouldn't be seen as too personal, but she hadn't been in the place long enough to get any ideas.

Clothes? Most men found them boring as a gift. There was a craft shop across the way and, knowing he would soon be back, she hurried inside.

Canvases, paints and brushes were put to one side for her with the arrangement that they would be delivered to her address some time during the next few days, and Nina emerged with the satisfaction of knowing that her gift to Rob would at least be something that appealed to him.

As she waited in the coffee-shop she was making plans. Providing that Eloise was no worse, would Rob share Christmas Day with them? she wondered. She'd been appalled to discover that he had no close family.

Obviously, he had friends. He was too popular in the village not to have, and he might have already been invited out for the day, but if she didn't ask she would never know.

He had the look on his face of a job well done when he came back and she eyed him curiously, but wherever he'd been he wasn't saying and she wasn't going to ask.

As the waitress put a coffee in front of him Nina voiced the thoughts that had been racing through her mind. 'Would you like to spend Christmas Day with us, Rob?'

He eyed her unsmilingly and her enthusiasm began to diminish. 'It's nice of you to ask, but do you think it a good idea, with Eloise's problems?'

'I think it would be a good idea no matter what,' she persisted.

His smile was gentle. 'In that case I'm delighted to accept…just as long as you let me help with the preparations.'

'No need,' she told him, her face lightening. 'Dad always cooks the turkey and I can do the rest as long as Eloise is there to keep an eye on me.'

As they drove home Rob's thoughts were sombre. Nina was clutching at straws. Desperate for a normal Christmas, she'd invited him to join them. He hoped that it would work out as she wanted.

'I know what you're thinking,' she said challengingly. 'That I'm playing at happy families.'

'Only because I hate to see you miserable.'

'I'm miserable about a few things.'

'Yes. Don't think I'm not aware of that, but nothing is ever as simple as we would like it to be.'

'Only if we make it complicated,' she retaliated. 'But don't let's spoil the evening, Rob. It's been nice to get away from everyone and everything.'

'Except me,' he said with a quizzical smile, and waited for a reply. But there was none forthcoming. Nina's eyelids were drooping and he thought that a combination of sleepless nights and the warmth of the car were sending his vibrant young assistant into slumberland.

Eloise's appointment at the oncology unit was for early Friday afternoon and so Nina had been there for morning surgery.

Rob had come into her consulting room as she was about to leave for home in the lunch-hour, and because the other doctors were hovering his voice was low as he said, 'Remember, Nina, whatever the news is, good or bad, I'm here.'

Her heart leapt at the words but it was only for a moment as he went on to say, 'The same applies to Eloise. Tell her, will you?'

'Yes, I'll tell her,' she said stiffly, and went on her way, wishing that the men in her life were more flexible.

The late surgery was over. The staff had all dispersed and Rob was about to go up to the flat when the phone on his desk rang. He knew it would be Nina, and he found himself tensing.

As she said his name she sounded out of breath and he said warily, 'Yes, Nina?' But when she spoke again he could tell that it was happy laughter coming over the line and her next words explained the reason for it.

'It's working!' she cried. 'The chemo is working, Rob! Eloise is in remission!'

'So the frailty and general depression were from the treatment rather than the illness,' he breathed as relief swept over him.

'Yes! Yes! Yes!' Nina chanted joyfully in his ear.

'And what does she have to say to that?'

'She's stunned. I don't think she's taken it in yet.'

'And your father?'

'Pretending he knew all along that this would happen.'

'Why don't I take you all out for a celebratory meal?'

'Eloise is asleep. She went straight to bed when we got in and was out like a light within seconds. The relief for her must be exquisite…and Dad won't come without her.'

'Which leaves you?'

'Yes, just me…and I can't think of anything I'd like better than to spend the evening with you. For the first time in months I'm free of dread, Rob!'

'I'll pick you up in a couple of hours, and in the meantime I'll book us in for a meal somewhere,' Rob said buoyantly, with his own gloom lifting and a crazy urge inside him to forget all about surgery ethics and a bad relationship.

The sparkle was back. Rob could tell the moment Nina got into the car. He said laughingly, 'I'd have thought that you'd have been ready to collapse into bed, too, after all the stress you've been under.'

She laughed across at him, her green eyes shining, her mouth curving invitingly, and it took him all his time not to stop the car and take her into his arms.

But tonight he didn't want any hole-in-the-corner embraces. He wanted to wine her and dine her first, and then…

'Where are we going?' she asked, snuggling down in the seat like a contented cat.

'I've made a reservation at an hotel way up in the hills,' Rob said, 'but if you'd rather we went into town I can ring through on the mobile and cancel it.'

Nina shook her head. 'No. I've grown accustomed to this place. I find the town too noisy these days.' She chuckled happily. 'I must be getting old.'

It was one of the happiest evenings of her life. The hotel was a converted manor house, ivy-covered and elegant, and the food and service were in keeping with the structure.

But what mattered most was that they were at ease with each other. There was harmony between them and Nina sensed that the night would take its course to an ending that would be a beginning, too. The start of a love affair that would last for ever.

As they drove back beneath the light of a winter moon Nina felt that her heart would burst with happiness. Rob hadn't said anything to make her think things were going to be any different between them, but she could tell by the way he looked at her that he was ready to forget the limitations he'd set upon himself and as for herself there was no limit to her joy.

For one thing Eloise had at worst got a reprieve, and at best a cure, and Rob was here beside her, driving her through the velvet night. She was almost tempted to pinch herself to see if she was awake.

He pulled up outside the surgery. Turning to her, he said, 'Here are the keys to the flat, Nina. Will you unlock the door while I park the car?'

There had been no need for him to issue an invitation. They both knew they were going to make love. Rob hadn't touched her all evening, but it hadn't mattered because she'd known what was to come.

When he took her in his arms the moment the door had closed behind them, she gladly gave herself up to the inevitability of the moment.

He undressed her with swift gentleness and then stood back to adore her slender nakedness. And after she had taken off his clothes with hands that trembled, Nina knew that her feelings for this man with the supple grace of the unclothed, attractive male were the most important thing in her life.

And later, much later, as he slept beside her, his face

tranquil, his broad chest moving gently up and down and one arm thrown across the covers, the memory of how they'd come together in a mixture of desire and tenderness made her tremble all over again.

Lying contentedly in the hollow of his back, the thought of the days to come with Rob beside her and Eloise gradually getting back her strength was pleasurable beyond description, and with a smile on her face she slid into sleep.

Nina awoke to find herself alone in a room full of pale sunlight. There was a note on the bedside table and as she reached out for it sleepily the words on it seemed to leap out at her.

Last night was wonderful, but it was a mistake. I should have known better. With Eloise on the way to recovery you're now free to take up your own pursuits, Nina. You've made it clear all along that you can't wait to get away from this place, and I don't want to be the one that you blame in later years for blighting your career.

I thought that I'd managed to put all the difficulties to one side, but this is something that has only come up since we heard the good news yesterday. I can't be responsible for keeping you here, and I'm ashamed that I put my longing for you before what will be best for you in the long run.

Maybe in a few years' time we might try again, but in the meantime the matter isn't up for discussion. I've made up my mind.

In case you're wondering where I've disappeared
to, it's my turn for Saturday surgery.

Love, Rob.

After the first few painful moments anger swept over
her. How could Rob make a decision of such magnitude
without consulting her? Who was he to decide what was
best for her? If she were given the chance to travel the
world over, from one continent to another, it would
mean nothing without him.

The matter wasn't up for discussion, he'd written.
Well, so be it. If he thought that he'd made the big
gesture he had another think coming. Nothing would
budge her from Stepping Dearsley as long as he was
there. She couldn't exist if he wasn't near her, but this
time he'd fobbed her off one time too many.

She wasn't going to beg. The next move, if any, had
to come from him and having made that decision, she
flung on her clothes from the night before and left the
building without going anywhere near the surgery.

It was the Saturday night of the practice Christmas party
at the hotel. Nina hadn't been sure whether she would
be going until the last minute as Eloise had been con-
fined to bed with a heavy cold for most of the day.

But in the early evening her stepmother came downstairs, and when she saw that Nina was making no attempt to get ready for the party she tried to shoo her up
to her room with the request that she put on her most
glamourous outfit and sally forth.

'I'm feeling much better,' she said convincingly, 'and
Rob is going to be disappointed if you aren't there.'

'I don't think so,' Nina said flatly. 'My absence would
probably be greeted with relief.'

'I can't believe that,' Eloise protested laughingly.

'He's accepted your invitation to share Christmas Day with us, hasn't he?'

'Yes, he has, but I'll believe he's coming when I actually see him here.'

'So matters aren't going well between you?'

Nina sighed. 'We'd just got over the aftermath of the Bettine business when we heard your good news, and now Rob won't have anything to do with me because he doesn't want to stand in the way of me doing what I've always wanted to do.'

'Going abroad, you mean?'

'Yes. He's heard me say so often that I didn't like being cooped up here that he now expects me to spread my wings and fly.'

'Well, there is nothing to stop you now, is there?' Eloise said gently. 'You wouldn't have been brought here in the first place if I'd had my way.'

'Yes, I know that,' Nina said huskily, 'but I couldn't have been anywhere else, knowing what you were facing. Dad was right to ask me to come back home...and now that I've got the chance to do my own thing, I don't want to go. Because I'm in love with Rob.'

'Have you talked it through?'

'No, because he says the subject isn't up for discussion.'

Eloise sighed. 'He's a good man and I can see his point of view, but he ought to give you the chance to put yours forward. I'm relieved to hear that he's got over his hang-ups with the Bettine business, but it seems a shame that no sooner is one problem sorted out than another presents itself. When is her baby due?'

Nina shrugged. 'I'm not sure. Some time in January, or maybe early February, I would imagine. We don't see much of her these days. Since her father-in-law died she's hardly ever around. We've been doing her surgeries between the four of us.'

'And what's her excuse?'

'Oh, I don't know. Pregnancy? Family commitments? I think she'll leave the practice soon.'

'And how will you feel about that?'

'Delighted. Although I don't think it will make Rob any more likely to want to plight his troth with another of the partners. But with regard to that I think he's expecting me to depart for war-torn parts at any second.'

'And you're not going to do that?'

'Not unless I'm convinced that there's absolutely no hope of us getting together.'

Eloise gave her a gentle push towards the stairs. 'Go and get ready and don't come down again until you are.'

The season's first covering of snow had been falling in silent white flakes since the early afternoon and by the time Nina was ready to leave for the party the village was a glistening winter wonderland.

Unaccustomed to the countryside at this time of year, she caught her breath as she stepped outside. The scene was like something from a Christmas card. What a pity that today wasn't the day. There were still two weeks to go until Christmas, and unless a very cold winter was on its way the soft white carpet would be long gone by then.

Her father had followed her outside and as she exclaimed at the beauty of the scene he said dourly, 'Aye. It looks all right, but with a fall such as this all the roads over the Pennines will be blocked. Folks have been known to freeze to death when they've been caught up on the tops in this sort of weather.'

'Dad!' she exclaimed. 'Don't spoil it with that sort of grim foreboding. Can't you look on the bright side for once? Think how much fun the children are going to have.'

She could hear shouting and laughter already from young voices farther down the road, and if she hadn't been dressed to kill she would have been tempted to join them. But an elegant, dark green trouser suit with the palest of lemon blouses was hardly the attire for snowballing.

Added to that, she had other plans for the evening that concerned a certain senior partner whom she was determined should be totally aware of her at the gathering of the practice staff.

'Robert Carslake won't be able to resist you tonight,' Eloise had said fondly when Nina had gone to give her a twirl before setting off.

'Don't underestimate the man,' Nina had said wryly. 'He's the sort who won't be sidetracked when he decides to do something.'

'He's also a man of honour,' Eloise had pointed out. 'There aren't many who would pass up the chance of marrying a beautiful girl like yourself for the reasons Rob has given.

'I know that coming back home was the last thing you'd envisaged doing and, as I've been anxious to point out, it wasn't at my insistence,' she said gently. 'But it's up to Rob to help you decide whether these last months have been just a blip in your life or a significant pause.'

'I've changed,' Nina said dreamily. 'The countryside has cast a spell over me. When I go to town these days I can't wait to get back.'

'Are you sure it's the countryside that holds you in thrall?' Eloise asked.

'You mean that it's Rob who's keeping me here? It's both, really. A bit of one and a lot of the other. But I could live in the Burmese jungle or at the North Pole if he were there.'

And now it looked as if she was, indeed, in the polar regions as frost glittered on the window-panes and snow crunched beneath the heavy winter boots that went oddly with her party clothes, but which would be discarded the moment she arrived at the Royal Venison.

CHAPTER NINE

BY THE time Nina reached the hotel it was snowing heavily again, and she remembered her father's comments. Down here in the village it was a delightful scene, but there could be danger for those travelling among the peaks if it kept up.

But once she was inside, with her boots discarded for a pair of high-heeled sandals and the festive warmth of the place reaching out to her, she forgot the snow and prepared to enjoy herself.

They were all there—Kitty Kelsall the cleaner, the receptionists, the two nurses, the practice manager and three of the four partners, along with all the rest of those who kept the village practice running smoothly.

Bettine was the only missing member and Nina couldn't help but feel relieved that Rob's ex-fiancée wasn't going to be eyeing them both with her cool stare.

It seemed fitting somehow that if Bettine couldn't turn up for the surgeries she shouldn't be at the Christmas party. But when Rob was questioned about her absence he said that she was intending to be there with them as her last appearance before bowing out of the practice.

'So you'll be looking for another partner,' Nina said after he'd made the announcement.

He'd nearly been late himself and his smile had been rueful when a cheer had gone up at his arrival.

'Sorry I'm late, folks,' he'd told them. 'I was called out to our first case caused by the snow. One of the old folks at The Laurels who's inclined to wander was

151

tempted outside into the gardens and slipped. Unfortunately, there wasn't a lot I could do. It was almost certainly a fracture of the femur and just a case of waiting for the ambulance.'

While he'd been speaking his glance had been on Nina, young, slender and elegant, standing amongst them with a glass in her hand. As if drawn by a magnet, he'd gone to her side, only to be surrounded by enquiries about Bettine's non-arrival.

It was after his news about Bettine's impending departure that Nina had wanted to know if he would be replacing her, and with his pulse quickening at her nearness he said, 'Yes, I will…and I think that next time I'll stay with my own sex.'

'Why?' she asked in surprise.

'Less hassle.'

He watched the light die out of her eyes.

'So you still have reservations about me?'

'Yes, I do, but not as a doctor. You're coming along nicely. It's my peace of mind that I have reservations about.'

Nina rolled her eyes heavenwards. 'Oh, please! Spare me the entrapment angle. I never go where I'm not wanted.'

'Who said you weren't wanted?' Rob parried, and added with sudden seriousness, 'It's possible to want something too much in this life, Nina.'

Before she could answer that thought-provoking comment the call went up that the meal was about to be served, and her pleasure at being with Rob increased when she found herself sitting next to him at the table.

Nina sensed that it wasn't accidental. Someone had taken the trouble to put place names out and had seated them next to each other. As she eyed the cards in front of them she saw amusement in Rob's dark gaze and asked, 'Who did the seating arrangements?'

'Not me,' he said with a smile. 'The hotel management asked for someone to call round this afternoon to sort out who was sitting where. The practice manager offered and here we are. As if I don't see enough of you as it is.'

She knew he was teasing but it hurt. Maybe deep down that was how he felt, that she was too often in his sight. Yet he'd just said that she had the makings of a good doctor. But that wasn't what he'd been referring to, was it?

With an answering smile she gave him a gentle push. Tonight, for a few brief hours, she was going to throw off the fraught mantle of misery that had been weighing her down ever since she'd awoken to find him gone.

If Rob was weary of the sight of her, it wasn't true on her side. He didn't accompany her on home visits now. She'd proved that she could be left to cope on her own and he'd wasted no time in letting her get on with it. That was gratifying in one way, but it meant that they spent less time together.

Of course, they saw plenty of each other at the practice—at meetings, between surgeries, in the various clinics, and coming and going generally as each day came and went. But the time they spent together there was nothing compared to sitting close beside him as they ate a festive meal.

When they got up from the table there was a cabaret and again they sat together, oblivious of the curious stares from some of the practice members.

How long Rob's preference for her company was going to last Nina didn't know, but tonight she was on a high. For just a short time she was secure inside a happy bubble of contentment and nothing was going to burst it.

There was still no sign of Bettine. The curiosity over her absence had died down and no further comments were made about her non-appearance.

But as the evening progressed and the party spirit throbbed among them, Rob glanced towards the door a few times. Nina wasn't sure whether he was watching out for Bettine or whether he was tuning in to the various telephone calls coming through to Reception.

The receptionist had seen him eyeing her through the open door of the restaurant and she came across. 'The roads over the Pennines are blocked,' she said worriedly. 'A coach party from Sheffield have cancelled their booking. It's still snowing heavily outside and traffic in the village is moving very slowly.'

Rob had been frowning as he'd listened to the impromptu weather forecast, and Nina thought they'd just been given the reason for Bettine's non-appearance. Yet it was only a short distance from the hall. Surely the roads weren't that bad.

The phone rang again and as the girl hurried to answer it Nina's reasoning proved wrong. 'It's for you, Dr Carslake,' she called across.

As Rob got to his feet and moved swiftly to the reception desk, Nina's precious bubble burst. And when he turned to her with a face from which all pleasure had been wiped clean, she knew that it wasn't good news that he had for her.

'It isn't the weather that's prevented Bettine from getting here,' he said when he came back to her. 'Complications have developed with the pregnancy. That was her husband on the phone. He's tried to get an ambulance but they can't get through. The drifts are too deep upon the tops.'

'She's at the farm!' Nina exclaimed as the evening disintegrated before her eyes.

'Yes. Unfortunately. And it doesn't sound good, but I can't tell what's wrong from just a phone call. I'll have to drive as far as I can and then, if the road is blocked, I'll do the rest on foot.'

Nina's jaw dropped. 'You're not going up there, surely?'

'I'm amazed to hear you say that,' he said abruptly. 'Of course I am!'

'But why does it have to be you?' she asked angrily as once again her father's grim predictions came to mind.

'Because it's me that she's asking for,' he said, becoming more aloof by the minute. 'I'm going home to change into some warm clothes and then I'll be off.'

'What's wrong?' Gavin asked as Rob went striding off into the winter night. 'Not an emergency, is it? Tonight of all nights.'

Nina nodded glumly. 'Yes. It's Bettine. Something's gone wrong with the pregnancy. They've called Rob out to the farm.'

Gavin shuddered. 'Rather him than me. It's cold enough to freeze a brass monkey out there. But you know what they say.'

'No, what do they say?'

'Old habits die hard. Remember they were engaged once.'

Her spirits sank even lower. 'You're not saying that he still cares, surely?'

He shrugged. 'Who's to say? Rob isn't the type to flit from bird to bird.'

Tell me about it, she wanted to say, but Gavin would zoom in on a comment of that nature and wouldn't rest until she'd explained what she'd meant.

'It's to be hoped he's got some good, strong boots handy,' he was saying, 'and a flask or, better still, a St Bernard.'

The mention of boots had given birth to an idea. Nina had the pair in the cloakroom and there was a warm jacket in her car.

Admittedly, she would be wearing the flimsy trouser suit underneath, but she'd be protected enough on top to go with him. She couldn't let him go alone. Eloise's problems were sorting themselves out, but if she lost Rob, what would there be to live for?

When he came dashing downstairs from the flat she was waiting for him, an incongruous figure with silk trousers tucked into boots and a bulky waterproof jacket that made the top half of her look twice as wide as the bottom.

'Nina!' he exclaimed. 'What are you doing here?'

'I'm coming with you.'

His face darkened. 'Oh, no, you're not!'

'Oh, yes, I am! Remember, I've been running the antenatal clinic in Bettine's absence, and what I don't know about the problems of pregnancy isn't worth knowing,' she said jokingly. 'So let's be off. The weather is too severe to waste time arguing.'

'The severity of the weather is why I don't want you with me.'

She was already thrusting herself into the passenger seat of his car, and as she eyed him defiantly through the falling snow he gave in.

'All right, but the first sign of any danger and you're turning back. Agreed?'

'Yes.'

The gritter had already been out in the main street of the village and on the road that led to the hills. For the first couple of miles the car made reasonable progress, but the bleak north wind that had sprung up was blowing the snow into drifts and they both knew it was only a matter of time before they were forced to stop.

If Bettine had been at the hall there would have been no problem. It was on the edge of the village, but the Blackmore farm was on a remote hillside and one of the homesteads that were always first to be cut off in bad weather.

Visibility was worsening by the minute, and as they turned a bend in the road the car ran into a drift.

'Damn!' Rob exclaimed as the wheels spun round ineffectually. 'We're only a mile away and this has to happen! There's a spade in the boot. I'll see if I can dig us out.'

As he opened the car door his face was as bleak as the weather. 'We've got to get to Bettine, Nina. There are all the signs of something very serious and she's up there with four useless men.'

'Where's her mother-in-law?'

'Gone visiting relatives,' he called over his shoulder as he fought his way round to the boot.

It was no use. As fast as he dug out the snow from around the car wheels it was as bad again. After ten minutes' fruitless effort he got back in the car.

'We're going to have to walk the rest of the way,' he said edgily, and with his voice rising he went on, 'Why I was stupid enough to let you come with me I'll never know. The situation we're in at the moment is that two of us are risking our lives, rather than just one. If anything happens to you it will be my fault.'

'It won't,' Nina said calmly. 'In case you haven't noticed—or aren't prepared to admit it—we're a team.'

'Is that so?' he commented grimly. 'Have you never heard the saying that he travels fastest who travels alone?'

'Does that refer to your private life…or the present moment?' she asked as she prepared to step out into the blizzard.

From where she was sitting it looked as if the only person he was bothered about was Bettine. As for herself, she had the impression that she was baggage he could have done without. Maybe Gavin had been right. Perhaps there was still some feeling there for his ex-fiancée.

Ignoring the comment, Rob was switching off the car engine and checking that all the windows were secure. Once it was done he said tightly, 'It's time we got moving or we're going to freeze to death. Out you go.'

As they stood beside the car Rob took her arm in a grip that would have had her yelping in less dire circumstances. Above the howling of the wind he cried, 'Hang onto me, Nina. We've a hard walk ahead of us.'

Every step was an effort, every breath torn from them as the wind cut like a knife. Nina's spirits had never been lower as they fought their way towards the farm.

She'd ventured into this dreadful weather on impulse to support Rob and had ended up putting him more at risk.

Added to that, she was miserable because Rob's concern over Bettine seemed to outweigh the normal GP's involvement with a patient. But Bettine wasn't just any patient, was she? He'd been engaged to the woman, for heaven's sake…and she was one of the partners at the practice.

His arm was around Nina's shoulders as they floundered in the snow, with the icy wind lashing at them. Under other circumstances she would have shrugged it off in her annoyance, but she had no option but to huddle against him as her legs in the soaking silk trousers got colder and colder.

With their heads bent against the wind she couldn't see his expression. If she had been able to Nina would have seen grim consternation in it.

He'd put her at risk by allowing her to come with him, Rob was thinking desperately. If either of them got out of this alive they would be lucky. The snow was drifting higher than ever at the sides of the road. Soon it would be impassable.

A dark shape loomed up in front of them suddenly and then there were others. The Blackmore brothers had come in search of them. Thank God! They must be nearly there.

Rob went straight to Bettine's room the moment he arrived, stripping off his wet outdoor clothes as he went. For Nina there were curt instructions to get into a hot bath and find herself something dry to wear, so it seemed that her presence wasn't required.

The youngest of the brothers sheepishly offered her a dressing-gown of his mother's and a pair of slippers that were three sizes too big. When she surfaced after the briefest of soaks, she found Rob trying to get through to the ambulance unit.

'There's no reply,' he said briefly. 'I hope that the wires aren't down.'

'What is it?' she asked. 'What's wrong with Bettine?'

His face was grey in the light of the candles that the farmers had resorted to when the weather conditions had affected the generator. For Rob to look like that he must still care for Bettine, she thought forlornly.

'I'm not sure,' he said tersely in answer to her question. 'We need to get her to hospital urgently. She needs a scan to pinpoint the problem. If I were asked to make a guess I'd say that the placenta has become detached.'

'Oh, no!' Nina breathed.

'Oh, yes, I'm afraid. Bettine is of the same opinion, although it isn't easy to make an unprejudiced diagnosis when you're the patient.'

'So what are the symptoms?'

He was still trying to get through on the phone and his reply was abrupt, his manner towards her still chilly.

'There's blood loss and the uterus is rigid and painful, which I think is due to pressure building up from bleeding behind the placenta. In normal weather she would be in hospital by now, but we've seen for ourselves how deep the snow is.

'Nothing is going to get through on the roads for the next few hours, or even days maybe. There's only one means of transport that will get her out of here, and if I can't get through to the ambulance station to request that they authorise it even that will be out of the question.'

'Helicopter?'

He nodded. 'Yes, by helicopter. The wind has dropped and the clouds are clearing. So it can get here, thank God.'

At that moment his face lightened and he called across, 'I'm through!' As he waited to be connected he said, 'Will you go to her? Tell her that I'm sorting something out.'

'Where's Bettine's husband?' Nina asked from the doorway.

'With her, of course!' he snapped.

Keith wasn't with his wife. She was alone when Nina went into the bedroom, and her first fretful words were, 'Where's Rob? I want him with me..'

'He's arranging for a helicopter to pick you up,' Nina told her.

Her smile was reassuring, but it hid a longing to tell Bettine that Rob didn't belong to her any more, that she'd put his life at risk by asking him to come out to this remote farm in horrendous weather.

The woman might be in a serious condition but she didn't own Robert Carslake, far from it. She'd forfeited all right to lay claim to him when she'd been unfaithful. If she'd been crying out for Rob all the time in her husband's presence, it was no wonder that he was absent.

As if reading her thoughts, Bettine said, 'If you're wondering where Keith is, he's bringing in the animals. Some of them are out on the hillside.'

Her eyes went to the window-ledge where the snow was piled high. 'When *they* give birth it's usually a simple thing. He can't understand why I'm not proving to be the same.'

Then he's not very supportive, Nina thought. No wonder Bettine is desperate to have Rob by her side. If ever she'd felt surplus to requirements it was now. He'd made it clear that he wished she'd stayed at home, and the woman in the bed wanted only him beside her. So what was she doing here?

And as if that feeling wasn't bad enough, there was panic inside her because she hadn't stayed where she had been needed. Would anyone have told her dad and Eloise where she was?

The moment the phone was free she must ring them to reassure the woman who was the exact opposite to this one. Eloise had grace and dignity and a great depth of kindness, while Bettine…

Rob was in the doorway with some of the tension wiped from his face. 'It's organised, Bettine,' he said. 'A helicopter with paramedics on board will be setting off in the next few minutes. I'm going to ask the Blackmore men if they'll try to clear a landing patch for it.'

'No! Don't leave me,' Bettine pleaded. 'Let *her* ask them.'

'Would you, please, Nina?' he asked. 'Explain what's required and tell them it needs doing without delay.'

She nodded woodenly. 'Her' was being sent on the errands. She didn't mind that in such an emergency, but did Bettine have to be so rude and demanding?

As Bettine was carried into the helicopter, with her husband now beside her, Rob and Nina stood to one side.

He'd impressed on the paramedics to watch for signs of shock due to blood loss and they'd taken careful note. It had been known to happen in such cases and was very serious if not treated.

With the pregnant woman's problems receiving attention, it was time for Nina to think about her own. She'd managed to get through to her father and felt weak with relief to hear that Eloise was all right, apart from being anxious about their safety.

And now, in a borrowed dressing-gown and slippers that were like canal boats on her feet, she was desperate to get back home.

As if Rob was tuned in to her anxiety he said, 'I've asked the helicopter crew to come back for us, otherwise we could be stuck here for days.'

'Good,' she said flatly, with sudden treacherous tears threatening.

He saw her expression and asked quickly, 'What is it, Nina?'

'I feel as if I've lost my way,' she sobbed.

Rob stared at her in consternation but made no move to touch her. 'I'm not sure if I get your meaning, but if you're referring to us being stuck out here, I've just said that I've asked them to come back for us.'

'That's not what I mean,' she choked. 'I'm talking about my life. I had it all planned. Once I'd got my degree I was going to work abroad as a free spirit. But I was sidetracked into Stepping Dearsley and now I don't know what I want.'

As Rob took a step towards her she waved him away and went on, 'Eloise thought my stay in the village could become a "significant pause" because I'd met you. That it would stand out as a special time that would change my life. Then again, she said that it might just be a blip that I would soon recover from and forget in no time.'

Rob's face seemed set in stone 'You say you've been sidetracked into coming here! I must be mistaken, then. I thought it was because you loved Eloise and wanted to be with her. Are you saying that you begrudge the time you're giving her?'

'No! Of course I don't. She means everything to me. What I'm trying to say is that you have me totally confused. I thought that you were attracted to me as much as I was to you. I was ready to respect your wish to have some breathing space after your engagement to Bettine. But you've kept me dangling long enough and today, after watching you drooling over her, I know why.'

'You're saying that you think I still care for her?'

'Right in one!'

'I'm a doctor, for heaven's sake. I would show concern over any patient as ill as she is. Jealousy is an unattractive emotion. You should try to curb it.'

There was a chill inside the farmhouse as well as outside, she thought miserably. She must have been insane to ever think anything would come of their relationship.

What had happened to the pleasant evening they'd been sharing together? And the night when they'd slept in each other's arms? It seemed like a lifetime since she'd thought they'd been in tune and the song a love song.

Tonight she was seeing another side of him. Bettine had beckoned and Rob had come running, taking no heed of anything except that she needed him.

Was she being unreasonable? She would have done the same if someone had sent for her in such circumstances, but in her case it wouldn't have been an ex-fiancée.

Nina brushed away the tears with the back of her hand and Rob's face softened, but she wasn't having any of it.

'I'm not jealous and I do appreciate how sick Bettine is, but it doesn't alter the fact that she still means something to you…and I don't!' she flared.

The kitchen door opened at that moment and what Rob would have said in reply was lost as the two younger Blackmores appeared with frost on their beards and snow on their boots.

'It's back,' one of them said. 'The helicopter's back.'

'Do you want to come with us?' Rob suggested.

'Naw,' he replied. 'Somebody has to see to the animals. We'll be all right. We've lived through worse weather than this.'

'I'm going to change back into my own clothes before I go home,' Nina told them. 'That is, if they're dry.'

They were. Feeling more like herself in the creased trouser suit, she flicked a comb through her hair and they were ready to go.

'I'll keep in touch with the hospital,' Rob told the two men, 'and maybe when your brother gets back he'll give me a ring.'

'That was just to let you see that Bettine's husband doesn't harbour the same sort of dark thoughts as you,' he said as they went outside into the cold night. 'He understands that she was only desperate to have me with her because I'm a doctor.'

'*He* isn't…wasn't…in love with you,' she shrieked.

'So it's in the past now, is it? That makes me think there couldn't have been much depth to your feelings.'

'You can think what you like. I don't care if I never see you again!'

'Thank God you're both safe!' Eloise breathed as Nina arrived home in time for Sunday breakfast. 'Where's Rob?'

'Gone home,' Nina informed her briefly.

'Should have brought him here,' her father said with his usual sparseness of speech. 'Enough ham and eggs to feed a regiment.'

'He can cook his own.'

'Oh! Do I detect a note of disharmony?' Eloise asked. 'And before you answer that question, how is Bettine Blackmore?'

'Not very well at all. Rob thinks that the placenta has come away.'

'And what do you think…Dr Lombard?' she asked gently.

'I didn't get a look in. She only wanted Rob.'

'And you weren't happy about that? She was pretty close to him, you know.'

'Yes, but it's in the past. You think I'm being unreasonable, don't you?'

'Just a bit, darling, but let's forget about that for the moment. I'm sure you must be longing to get out of those crumpled clothes. Do you want to change first or eat?'

'Eat, I think. The smell of the food is too tempting. No one can cook breakfast like Dad.'

Nina had been observing Eloise ever since she'd got back, watching for signs that she'd been overdoing it, but at that moment she seemed well enough.

She felt as if she'd been away for an eternity, but it was only just over twelve hours since she and Rob had left the party, long enough, though, for her to have finally seen sense. Once Christmas was over Rob Carslake wouldn't see her heels for dust.

She could go with an easy mind now. Her father and Eloise would cope now that Eloise had been given the all-clear, and maybe in time she would forget what had been such a significant pause in her life.

Rather than changing after she'd eaten, Nina went to bed, feeling weary in mind and body. She'd told Rob she had no interest in seeing him again, but she really didn't have a choice. Monday morning would arrive all too soon. The duties of the village practice would throw them together whether she liked it or not, and at that moment it was a depressing thought.

The bedside phone rang as she was drifting into sleep, and when she answered it Rob's voice came over the line. The helicopter had dropped them off on the village green and before he'd been able to say anything she had departed, a bedraggled figure in her dried-out clothes.

He was butting into her life again. What did he want this time?

'Nina?' he said.

'Yes?'

'Just checking to make sure you're not suffering any ill effects from the cold.'

'It all depends which cold you're referring to,' she said, her voice slurred with sleep. 'The chill that *you* were giving off, or the weather?'

'So you're still travelling that road? Punishing me for doing my job.'

'*I'm* the one who's being punished,' she retorted, 'but I was too dim to see it until today.'

'I'm not going to argue with you, Nina,' he said levelly. 'You're half-asleep for one thing. But before I ring off, do you want to hear the latest about Bettine…or not?'

'Of course I do,' she said indignantly. 'I might have been the bystander out there at the farm, and be suffering from what you describe as jealousy, but I was just as concerned as you about her condition.'

'All right, you've convinced me. As for the rest of it, you might be in a more reasonable frame of mind when you've had some sleep.'

'Don't bank on it!'

He ignored her sarcasm and said in a milder tone, 'They've done a Caesarean section to relieve the bleeding and to prevent the detachment of the placenta getting any worse. She went into shock while they were transporting her and it was panic stations for a while.'

'And the baby?' she breathed.

'A boy. He's six weeks premature so he won't be coming home in a hurry but, considering all that went on, he's fine.'

There was silence and Nina sensed that there was more to come. She wasn't mistaken. 'Before you hear it from anyone else, they're going to call him…Robert,' he said evenly, and as she gazed speechlessly into the receiver he rang off.

CHAPTER TEN

THE weekend's weather brought in a spate of coughs and colds to Monday morning's surgery, and all four doctors were kept busy.

There'd been a case of hypothermia too. Old Mrs Dobson, who lived in a cottage at the bottom of the hill road, had been found in a distressed state by her home help and Rob had gone out to her before the start of surgery.

He'd been discussing the old lady with Vikram when Nina arrived, and, after giving her a brief nod, had gone on with what he was saying.

'The lady was drowsy, confused and her heartbeat and breathing were lowered,' he was explaining.

'So you've had her hospitalised?' Vikram asked.

Rob nodded, his thoughts switching channels as the sight of Nina's set face put the seal on what looked like being a depressing day.

Yet, whatever the atmosphere between them, he knew he should be thankful. They might have ended up as two more cases of hypothermia or, worse, cold and stiff on a mortuary slab, because the weather they'd battled against on Saturday night had been awful. If the Blackmore men hadn't appeared when they had, they could have been lost in the snow, buried beneath the high white drifts.

And what had he done? Told her off for being there with a noticeable lack of tact and gentleness. Maybe if he'd behaved differently, Nina wouldn't have read all

169

the wrong things into the way he and Bettine had been with each other.

But he'd been frantic, horrified that he'd let his mutinous young partner become involved in such a dangerous mission. Finesse had been the last thing he'd been capable of showing.

Vikram was eyeing him questioningly and Rob dragged his thoughts back to the present.

'Yes. I had the patient admitted to hospital,' he said. 'The paramedics wrapped her in space blankets and off they went. She was pretty bad and it's hard to understand how she could let herself get into that state. The house has plenty of heating and the old lady isn't impoverished.'

'It's a state of mind,' one of the practice nurses said. 'I know Jane Dobson and she keeps a tight hold on her purse-strings. I've seen her huddled in a blanket many a time on cold days, instead of putting the heating on.'

'Yes, well, this time it was nearly a catastrophe,' Rob said soberly. 'In fact it might still be if they don't get her body heat up pretty smartish.'

By the time they'd finished discussing Mrs Dobson Nina was already greeting her first patient, and Rob had no choice but to do the same.

Andy Jones was a hard worker and a hard drinker, and this morning he had a big toe that was making him wilt with agony.

'It started over the weekend, Doctor,' he told Nina, 'right out of the blue, and it's been killing me ever since. I'm only thirty-two. A bit young for rheumatism, don't you think?'

'There's no special age for that kind of thing,' she told him as he dragged off his sock, 'but in your case, in view of the amount of pain and the fact that it seems all round the joint of the toe, I'd say that here we have a case of gout.'

His jaw dropped. 'Gout! I thought only rich folk had that.'

She laughed, amazed that she had it in her to do so as the sight of Rob chatting amiably with the staff had done nothing to lift the gloom that had never left her since the helicopter had landed her safely back home.

'Don't you believe it. It's more likely to be caused by a high level of uric acid in the blood. You need to stay off liver and other kinds of offal and watch the drinking. Continued attacks of gout can affect the kidneys, sometimes to a serious degree. Right?'

He sighed. 'Yep.'

'I'm going to prescribe non-steroidal anti-inflammatory tablets. They should reduce the pain and take away the inflammation, but you will have to watch what you eat and drink or another attack could follow.'

He nodded towards the crowded waiting room. 'Why couldn't I just have a cough or a cold, like that lot in there? I can take or leave the liver, but I do like a drink.'

Nina shrugged. 'The solution is in your own hands, and if you don't cut down on the drinking I'll assume that the pain isn't as bad as you make out.'

He gave a reluctant smile. 'Oh, it's bad all right. I'm not kidding about that.'

'Well, there you are, then.'

Andy Jones had been wrong about everyone in the waiting room having coughs and colds. There were plenty who had, but not all of them.

In the middle of the morning Nina was faced with a smart, middle-aged housewife who was complaining of a very inflamed ankle.

She was limping as she walked across the room, and

went on to explain that she'd just been abroad and had been bitten by some sort of insect in the affected spot.

'I didn't see what it was,' she said. 'I just felt the bite or sting and hoped that it wasn't going to be trouble. But, as you can see, Doctor, that's exactly what it's ended up as. I know that the infection is getting worse as I can hardly walk.'

The ankle was inflamed. It looked red and angry and Nina hesitated about what to do. If there was poison there it needed to be released, and as she studied it carefully she decided that another opinion seemed to be called for.

'Yes, Nina. What can I do for you?' Rob asked with crisp brevity when she went to see him.

'I have a patient that I'd like you to see,' she said stiffly.

'Oh! Why? What's the problem?'

He was on his feet and motioning for her to lead the way.

'It could be a tick bite,' he suggested, after examining the ankle. 'But there doesn't appear to be anything embedded in the flesh. We'll give you some antibiotic cream and you should come back later for another check-up.'

The woman shuddered. 'Thank you, Doctor.'

'Thanks for sitting in on that one,' Nina said after the woman had gone, returning to a tone of chilly politeness.

'That's what I'm here for,' Rob replied in a similar tone. 'Amongst other things.'

Nina didn't rise to the bait. She would dearly have liked to, but there was a black cloud hanging over her and she couldn't see it lifting in the near future.

Not so for the rest of the staff of Stepping Dearsley Practice. The Saturday night party had put them in the

Christmas mood, and with the backwash from that and the news that Bettine had given birth to a son the atmosphere was light-hearted and forward-looking.

If the senior partner and his young trainee were on a lower level of good humour it was put down to the fact that they'd had a traumatic weekend. For hadn't they been fighting their way through a blizzard while the rest of them had been enjoying themselves?

The woman with the tick bite came back in the afternoon and the good news was that her ankle was already responding to the antibiotic cream.

When she'd gone there was an awkward silence between Nina and Rob. It was quieter now than it had been during their brief meeting that morning. The practice had been so busy then that they wouldn't have had the time to talk even if they'd wanted to, but now there was a lull. The number of patients had dwindled to a mere trickle.

The phone on the desk rang at that moment, and as he reached out for it Rob said, 'I've asked Reception to put me through to the Infirmary. I want to know if Jane Dobson's hypothermia is reducing.'

There was silence as he listened to the voice at the other end, and when he'd replaced the receiver he said, 'She's warming up. It's lucky we caught it in time, but the experience won't have done her any good.'

Nina nodded, still with the feeling that she had nothing to say to him, but it seemed as if Rob wasn't stuck for words.

'How is Eloise?' he asked.

'Improving slowly,' she said quietly.

He smiled. 'That's good. Very good indeed! Cancer is a strange thing. Two people can be given the same treatment. One will respond, and the other won't. Fortunately, in her case she is one of those who has.'

His face suddenly tightened and when Nina didn't reply, he went on, 'I suppose you'll be making plans to carry on with your interrupted career now? If that's the case, please remember that we shall require adequate notice at the practice.'

Rob's manner was infuriating her. How could he discuss something that affected them both so keenly in such a mundane manner? He was talking about her departure from Stepping Dearsley as if it were no more important than the weather!

'I'm not going anywhere until after Christmas,' she told him flatly. 'I want to spend it with Dad and Eloise. Once it's over I'll start making my plans.'

'So you're going to be here over Christmas, then?' he said, and she dared to hope that it was pleasure she heard in his voice.

'Yes,' she told him, and couldn't resist adding, 'Especially as you've just reminded me that I have to work a suitable notice.'

Her voice had thickened as treacherous tears threatened, and she bent her head. How could they be holding this conversation? she thought wretchedly. Since she'd arrived in the village they'd become friends, then lovers on that wonderful night, and now what were they? Polite strangers? And all because Robert Carslake was a man of principle.

Nina's head came up slowly and behind the tears that hung on her lashes Rob saw the misery in the beautiful green eyes. He knew why it was there, but he couldn't forget that she'd been brought to Stepping Dearsley at the command of her father and there was no way that he wanted to be the cause of any further manipulation in her young life.

Admittedly, Nina had made the move willingly because of her love for Eloise, but he wasn't going to ask her to sacrifice herself again on his behalf. She was a clever, vibrant woman and even if *his* life was committed to this 'rural backwater', he couldn't insist that hers should be, too.

And yet Nina was in his blood. She came into his every waking thought. Right from that first day when she'd come into contact with the paint pot he'd been entranced by her.

In the normal course of events he would have given himself a long breathing space after breaking up with Bettine, but what had happened? Nina had been there before he'd had the chance to get his balance. It had been a case of right person, wrong time.

He'd never got it quite right with her, and after the fiasco of the Bettine episode up at the hill farm he'd heard the death knell of their relationship start tolling.

The tears were glistening on her cheeks, and as he looked down on to her parted lips Rob gave in to the hunger that took hold of him every time she was near.

His kiss was gentle at first, more to comfort than in desire, but as Nina's mouth came to life beneath his the moment changed and passion took over. A raw need on both their parts was blotting out all other emotions.

As his mouth went to the hollow of her throat and the hand resting possessively on the bottom of her spine curved her inwards to rest against his hard loins, Nina knew that if they'd been anywhere else they would have made love again.

Or was she presuming too much? Her tears had melted the heart of the man of stone for a brief moment. But it wasn't going to last, was it? He was already putting her from him.

'I'm sorry, Nina,' he said flatly. 'Your tears made me forget my scruples.'

'Don't make excuses, Rob!' she flared. 'You're still playing hard to get, aren't you? I *am* distressed! I *do* need comfort! But I need you most of all. When will you ever see that?'

At that moment Gavin popped his head round the door to say that the practice nurse and the duty midwife were ready to start the Monday afternoon antenatal clinic, and as the fraught moment shattered Nina told him bleakly that she was on her way.

She had never felt less like it. Not only because of what had just happened between herself and Rob, but because of her dealings over the weekend with another pregnant woman who was now the mother of a small boy, to be named...Robert.

Fortunately Bettine and her child had survived the dangers of the detached placenta and were now in a stable condition. But it could have been so much worse, and as Nina dealt with the women gathered for their weekly check-ups she prayed that there would be no such dilemmas facing any of them, either now or in the future.

Most of them were doing fine, but Amanda Benson had a problem. A forty-year-old mother of two teenagers, and eight weeks pregnant, she had decided over the weekend that she wanted a termination.

She was weepy and almost incoherent as she explained that the baby hadn't been planned and she couldn't face the prospect of looking after it.

'Why have you suddenly changed your mind, Amanda?' Nina asked carefully as the woman in front of her mopped her eyes with a tissue. 'When I saw you last you were over the moon at the thought of another baby.'

'Yes, well, I've had time to think it over and I've decided that I'm too old to start again.'

'What does your husband think about your change of mind?'

'All he's concerned about at the moment is whether he'll be able to get another job,' she said flatly. 'He was made redundant on Friday.'

'I see. So it's the uncertain future that has made you decide on a termination? Not so much your age?'

Amanda shuffled uncomfortably in her seat. 'He'll go mad when he knows what I'm asking for,' she admitted. 'I haven't told him yet as he's got enough on his mind. But you do see, don't you, Doctor, that it's the sensible thing to do?'

'It might seem like that at the moment,' Nina agreed, 'but what about long term? You don't want to spend the rest of your life regretting it, do you? Go home and discuss it with your husband, but don't be too long. When you've gone into it more thoroughly, come back and let me know what you've decided. We'll take it from there.'

Leaving the nurse and the midwife to clear away at the end of the clinic, Nina went back to her room. As she slumped wearily into the chair behind her desk, Rob appeared in the doorway.

His face was grave and her heart sank. She hadn't been relishing the thought of seeing him again after her earlier abandon in his arms, but this was obviously something serious.

He took her long winter coat off the peg and held it

out to her without speaking. As she eased her arms into the sleeves his hand brushed her cheek for a moment.

'What is it? Where are we going?' she asked quickly, controlling the urge to grasp the capable hand and hold onto it for ever.

But they'd gone through that scenario once today and it had ended how it always did when they touched—a current that surged and then dimmed only too quickly.

'You'll see,' he promised with the beginning of a smile. 'And, Nina...'

'Er...yes?'

'Maybe next time you won't be in such a hurry to offer.'

He'd been propelling her towards the door, but now she stopped and told him decisively, 'I'm not budging until you tell me what's going on.'

'It's the cats!'

'Cats?'

'Ethel's cats. She's had a fall and has been taken to hospital with suspected fractures. Maybe you recollect your hasty promise that you and I would take care of them in such an event?'

She began to laugh. 'Yes, I do. But poor Ethel! How is she?'

'Not too good. She's in a lot of pain, but she was with it enough to remind me of our arrangement—or should I say your arrangement. After refusing to move until I'd assured her that we would do our duty, she finally let them put her in the ambulance. I've got a key, so shall we go and collect the moggies?'

With the feeling that the day was turning out to be a strange mixture of health care, misery, passion and black comedy, she nodded her agreement and followed him out onto the street.

The last thing she'd ever expected was that they would be landed prematurely with Ethel's cats, and she could see that Rob had his reservations about the situation. She supposed that two cats and a dog was rather a menagerie for a busy doctor to keep in the flat above the surgery and that some sort of compromise might be due.

'Shall I take three of them and you have the odd one?' she offered as they let themselves into Ethel's small cottage. 'After all, I did rather wish them upon you.'

He was stroking the nearest of the cats as it purred round his ankles. 'Feeling guilty, are we?' he said with dry amusement.

'Just a bit,' she admitted.

Rob shook his head. 'No, we'll leave it as it is. Ethel won't like it if we don't do it according to how she wants it. But I insist that you phone tonight to see how well they're settling in at my place...because if they don't, you, my sweet Nina, will be in big trouble.'

When Nina rang the first time there was no answer, but at a second try Rob was there.

'I've just got back from the hospital,' he explained with a note of constraint in his voice, and she wondered if he'd been visiting Bettine.

Not necessarily as the ex-fiancée. Perhaps more in the guise of the caring doctor who had battled through the blizzard to get to her. Whatever role he was adopting, if that was where he'd been, she didn't want to know.

'So how are Tiddles and Titmarsh behaving?' she enquired obediently. 'My two have settled in a treat.'

'Well, they would, wouldn't they. I have to be the one with the wanderers.'

'What do you mean?'

'I've been to rescue Titmarsh off Ethel's doorstep three times.'

'You're obviously not talking to them right,' she said laughingly, happy that they were communicating, even if it was only about their foster-cats.

'Maybe,' he agreed in a similar light tone, and then spoiled the moment by saying, 'If Ethel is still incapacitated when you're ready to leave for pastures new, what will you do?'

'Eloise and Dad will perhaps look after them.' *And stop pushing me to go!* she wanted to cry.

She wanted to stay. Stepping Dearsley had caught her in its pretty rural web, and even if it hadn't, the fact that Rob Carslake lived there would have been enough to hold her captive.

But she'd presumed too much on that score. He was attracted to her. She'd no doubts about that. But he wasn't exactly falling over himself to do anything about it and she would be a fool if she didn't move on.

'I'll come over and see if I can calm your wanderer down,' she offered, half hoping he would say no, but he took her up on it.

'Yes, do. I think that the poor thing is missing a woman's touch.'

As she threw a warm jacket over the pale green mohair jumper and tight black trousers into which she'd changed on arriving home, Nina was wishing that Rob would admit that he, too, needed a woman's touch—such as her own, for example.

What am I doing here…where I'm not wanted? she thought as she rang his doorbell. I've come round on an excuse and I'm amazed that Rob didn't see it for what it is.

A grey blanket of weariness, stemming from the day's

toil and emotions, suddenly settled on her and she leaned weakly against the doorpost.

'What's wrong?' Rob asked when he opened the door to her. 'You look exhausted.'

He led her inside and settled her in a chair in front of the fire. 'Let me get you a drink. Tea? Coffee? Sherry?'

'A sherry might liven me up a bit,' she said apologetically.

As he poured the drink Nina looked around her. The flat didn't look so basic tonight. There was a spruce in the corner, decorated with bright ornaments and coloured lights, and Christmas cards were everywhere, adding their own festive touch to the room.

Nina wished she could stay there for ever, secure and warm with Rob fussing over her. Perhaps in that moment he was seeing her as a patient.

She needed treatment, that was a fact. Treatment for the heartache and uncertainty that went with loving him, but he didn't seem to be tuned into her need.

As she slowly sipped the drink the heat of the fire was making her drowsy, and she was mortified when her eyelids became so heavy that she couldn't keep them open. What a state to be in when she had Rob all to herself, she thought as she tried to fight off sleep.

He was smiling as he watched her go over the edge into oblivion. Flaking out like that was the last thing she would want to do in case she missed something, but it was quite clear that she was worn out and, curled up in front of the fire, fast asleep, his trainee looked young and defenceless.

Yet somehow Nina looked as if she belonged there in his home. Not because a sparsely furnished flat above a doctor's surgery was the right habitat for her, but because where one of them was the other needed to be also.

Rob's face was sombre in the firelight as he looked down at her. It wasn't the right time for that sort of thinking. But he knew that he hadn't given Nina a chance to say her piece.

For a very good reason… He wasn't sure that his determination would hold in the face of hearing what she had to say. Just as he didn't know how he was going to endure life without her if she went off to some far land.

He bent and picked her up in his arms, handling her as gently as a mother would a child. Walking through into the bedroom, he laid her carefully on top of the bed.

She stirred and gave a gentle moan, but she didn't awaken. Covering her with the quilt, he sat beside her and gave himself up to serious thought.

CHAPTER ELEVEN

NINA awoke to find herself lying beneath a strange ceiling. Startled, she lay rigid as she sought to remember where she was. Then she turned her head and saw Rob lying beside her on top of the bedcovers, and it all came back.

She'd fallen asleep in front of the fire and he must have carried her into his bedroom. Her sigh was heartfelt. They'd spent the night together and she hadn't even known.

The weight over her middle was his arm, thrown across her in sleep. Lifting it carefully, she laid it across his chest.

He was deeply asleep, wearing just a pair of shorts, while she was still in the green jumper and black trousers.

With her eyes on the face that was never out of her mind, Nina began to strip off. She was desperate for a shower, even though it would mean putting on the same clothes again.

When she was down to her bra and pants she went to seek out the bathroom, and was about to investigate the shower when she remembered that the night before she'd told her father she was popping out for a few minutes. That had been twelve hours ago.

She smiled. He would have sounded reveille and she wouldn't have been there! A good excuse would be needed to explain her absence.

She could hardly tell him she'd spent the time with

Rob Carslake. Maybe she could invent an emergency that had taken up the night.

'All right,' her father commented when she'd said her piece. 'I'll expect you when? Nine hundred hours?'

'Yes,' she confirmed weakly. 'I'll be home by then.'

As she was replacing the phone Nina heard footsteps padding across the bedroom, and before she could beat a swift retreat Rob was there, leaning against the door-post.

'So you're awake,' he said, with the eyes that she'd once likened to winter chestnuts observing her semi-nakedness.

'Er...yes, I am,' she said with a husky laugh as the moment began to take hold of her. 'I thought you were still asleep.'

'Obviously,' he said softly as he moved towards her, 'but I'm not, am I? I've had someone warm and sweet-smelling beside me all night, and the moment she was gone I was lost.'

This isn't happening, Nina told herself. I'm not going to find myself in paradise twice. At any moment Kitty Kelsall will be clanking round with her bucket and mop, or Rob will be called out.

She took a step back, wrinkling her pert nose as she did so. 'I don't know about smelling sweet. I've just taken off the clothes that I'd been wearing for far too long and was about to have a shower.'

Rob was laughing. 'You'd smell sweet if you'd just come crawling out of the manure heap at one of the farms but, as you're concerned about it, how about us showering together?'

Her eyes were huge. 'I don't believe this is happening. You're being nice to me. Treating me as if I haven't got something catching. What's changed?'

The laughter left him. There was a look on his face that made Nina catch her breath.

'Last night when you were asleep I realised that you were where you belonged. Here with me. That from now on, where we go we go together. I'd been telling myself that it was the wrong time to tell you how much I love you when I'd only just broken with Bettine, but I'd finally laid that ghost to rest and was ready to move forward when Eloise got the all-clear.

'It was wonderful news, but the timing was wrong again, as the way was then open to you to work abroad as you'd longed to do. But I can't hold out any longer, Nina. I love you! Adore you! I want to make babies with you and cherish you for the rest of your life. So what are we going to do?'

'We're going to stay here in Stepping Dearsley until our children are grown and you're ready to leave the practice. Then we'll do the other thing…together,' she said softly. 'Agreed?'

He nodded. 'Yes. I don't have to be a GP for ever. We'll do as you say. One day, we'll take our skills to another country where they need us.'

As they frolicked in the shower, adoring each other's nakedness, bewitched by the magic the day had brought, Nina gave a gasp of comic dismay.

'What's wrong?' he asked.

'My dad! I said I'd be home by nine o'clock. He'll have me down as absent without leave…and what about Titmarsh? I was supposed to be giving him rehousing counselling!'

'I have a message from one of your expectant mums,' Rob said when Nina ran out to greet him on Christmas morning.

'Really? Which one?'

'Amanda. She told me to tell you that she's carrying on with the pregnancy. Apparently, her husband is a joiner and has decided to start his own business which, I'm sure we both agree, is positive thinking for a man who has lost his job.'

He smiled down at her in the circle of his arms. 'I told her that we might have some work for him.'

'We might? In what way?'

'Building our own house, maybe?' he said, and planted a kiss on the end of her nose.

Her eyes were as bright as emeralds. 'Really?'

'Yes, really. And I've got the very thing to hang on the walls.'

'What?' she asked, with the wonder still on her.

'You remember when we went into the town the other week and I said I had some business to see to?'

'Yes, of course. I wondered what it was.'

He was opening the boot of his car and he lifted out a big, flat package, loosely wrapped. Handing it to her, he said, 'I took this to be framed.'

'What is it?'

He laughed. 'Unwrap it and you'll see.'

'It's me!' she cried. 'You've painted me! Oh, Rob, I'm not that beautiful.'

'You are to me,' he said. 'It was my solace on the long, dark nights when my stupid pride kept me away from you…and now I can't believe it. I've got you both.'

MILLS & BOON®

Makes any time special™

**Mills & Boon publish 29 new titles
every month. Select from...**

Modern Romance™   Tender Romance™

Sensual Romance™

Medical Romance™   Historical Romance™

MAT2

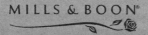

MILLS & BOON®

Medical Romance™

TOUCHED BY ANGELS *by Jennifer Taylor*

Dalverston General Hospital

Meg's healing touch could bring hope to the people of Oncamba, but she despaired of ever getting through to Jack Trent. As the image of his flighty ex-wife, she had enough trouble convincing him she was up to the job in hand...

PRACTISING PARTNERS *by Joanna Neil*

Helping Ross out at his busy practice suited Jenna, as her great new job didn't start for several weeks. This simple arrangement became complicated however when she realised her feelings for Ross were as strong as ever...

A FATHER FOR HER CHILD *by Barbara Hart*

Not wanting to spoil their happiness, Nurse Trudi Younghouse has not told Dan that little Grace was a surrogate baby. A conversation with Dan suggests he is against surrogacy and Trudi is in a dilemma—should she tell him at all?

On sale 2nd March 2001

FREE!
4 Books
and a surprise gift!

We would like to take this opportunity to thank you for reading this Mills & Boon® book by offering you the chance to take FOUR more specially selected titles from the Medical Romance™ series absolutely FREE! We're also making this offer to introduce you to the benefits of the Reader Service™—

- ★ FREE home delivery
- ★ FREE gifts and competitions
- ★ FREE monthly Newsletter
- ★ Books available before they're in the shops
- ★ Exclusive Reader Service discounts

Accepting these FREE books and gift places you under no obligation to buy; you may cancel at any time, even after receiving your free shipment. Simply complete your details below and return the entire page to the address below. *You don't even need a stamp!*

YES! Please send me 4 free Medical Romance books and a surprise gift. I understand that unless you hear from me, I will receive 6 superb new titles every month for just £2.49 each, postage and packing free. I am under no obligation to purchase any books and may cancel my subscription at any time. The free books and gift will be mine to keep in any case.

MIZEB

Ms/Mrs/Miss/Mr ....Initials..
BLOCK CAPITALS PLEASE

Surname..

Address..

....

....Postcode ....

Send this whole page to:
UK: The Reader Service, FREEPOST CN81, Croydon, CR9 3WZ
EIRE: The Reader Service, PO Box 4546, Kilcock, County Kildare (stamp required)